Islands of the Mind

Morgan's Knot – A Serial Fantasy
Episode VI

By

Eric Thomas Stiller, Jr.

For Leo

Islands of the Mind

Morgan's Knot – A Serial Fantasy
Episode VI

By

Eric T. Stiller, Jr.

Adrian was mesmerized by the serene intensity smoldering in the ancient *seer's* eyes. Orana's words echoed around the stonewalls of the cave like thunder rippling through the darkness, the tones and syllables reverberating in a strange hypnotic rhythm in his mind, "It is good that you believe in yourself and have a strong spirit, you will need it."

The young *seer* bowed his head, accepting the inadequacy of his powers. In spite of the lessons that allowed him to survive, he was acutely aware that he was a student sitting at the Master's knee. There was little doubt that the imminent instruction would push him beyond the challenges he encountered on his short but furious journey into the secrets and the Powers, including his skirmishes with Zepallo. Visions of dark caverns and evil creatures crept through his imagination and he struggled to push those terrors back into the shadows.

It was not that he was frightened of imminent nightmares, rather, the anticipation primed him to reach into that well of inner strength that loosed a rush of adrenaline coursing through his system. The hairs on the back of his neck bristled and his muscles tensed, his body ready to spring. All of his senses were open, prepared to collect information, aware of everything around him…the trickling of running water, the emblem on the wall, the echo of birds singing softly, the rhythm of his own breathing and the thumping of his heart beating in his chest, the quiet crackle of the fire, the beam of light streaming through wispy pinion smoke, the glowing pink aura, a bloated feather boa surrounding Orana's diminutive frame, and wise passion in her emerald eyes.

He could feel her energy swaddling him in a warm embrace but her spirit was burrowing into his soul and he knew there was nothing he could hide from this woman.

"Ah, you feel it, don't you?"

Adrian raised his head and met her stare.

"You feel those chemicals churning through your body. Every sense is primed to take in everything around you…sounds, smells, temperature, the movement of the air across your skin, the taste of the tea that lingers on the palette, the texture and rhythm of the energies, and the slivers of light flowing into this dark chamber. If there was movement anywhere close by, you would know instantly whether it was a threat or incidental. Your heart is beating rapidly and your mind is totally in tune with your surroundings. You can feel our auras exploring each other, yet, although we are the only people in this cave, you're uncomfortable."

"It isn't so much that I'm frightened, it's more a sense of anticipation of the unknown, because I have no idea of what's coming next," replied Adrian, quietly.

"The object of your instruction is to multiply these sensations by an infinite scale, touching not only your immediate surroundings but the entire world through all the planes, and then to teach you to synthesize your conclusions to produce something useful. Some of the situations you'll encounter will be frightening but understand that the only enemies that you'll have to defeat are the demons already living inside your soul. I understand that you were raised to be a nice young man but I also know that, given the choice between fight or flight, your instinct is to stand up for what you believe in and your gift is that you will always see the steps before you…even blindfolded and bound, you will find the path." She paused, "Consider the next few days as your opportunity to take a grand spiritual voyage, making excursions to various islands of your mind.

I had the advantage of knowing that I was a *seer* from the moment I was born. You, on the other hand, wasted the formative years of your life, through no fault of your own, but we'll have to go back to the beginning to teach you things you should already know!"

Before Adrian could reply, Orana melted and the cave disappeared. He found himself sitting crossed-legged on a smooth, open plain and he was completely naked.

The young *seer* gazed around a white world sweeping into the horizon, merging into the sky and the source of the brilliant light radiating from all directions. There were no sounds, no smells, no taste, and nothing to touch. The warm air was not moving and there was nothing that might offer a sense of scale or direction. Even the ground beneath him had no texture. It was simply flat.

Resting his hands on his knees, palms up, he drifted into the meditative state that he learned from Simian. He opened his inner senses, exploring his surroundings, and recognized that he was truly alone in a world that had yet to be created. Perhaps the first lesson was to fashion his surroundings with the things that were most dear, the world as he might design it.

Before he could concentrate on that single thought, his entire life flashed across the white sky like a spiraling coil of film, each frame a scene, a moment, and it was all happening in reverse. He saw his friends, his fellow *seers*, the animals and their plane, the battle on the island, Ponte's library and the Golden Crystal, the House of the Four Seasons, the inside of the lairs of the Dark Forces and the pulsing red *orb* that had held his spirit captive, the Wailing Wall and the Basilica in Rome, the Island of the Children and the world under the sea, and all of his challenges and adventures from the first day he arrived on the Morgan's Knot. Farther back, his memories roamed through his home on the bay, the children who attended his school, the sensation of piloting a sailboat, his father's strength, and his mother's warm embrace.

He could see every detail of his bedroom, his favorite toys, his books, and his teddy bear lying on his red bedspread. The salt air blowing in from the bay billowed the curtains like the veils of angels, as his mother used to whisper as she cradled him in the rocking chair, and the morning sun created long feathers of gold that crept across the blue carpet on the floor. Suddenly, he was an infant with no cares in the world other than being safe, warm, and well fed.

He opened his eyes and took in the endless white plain, bare to the horizon in every direction, except, in the distance, he could see a small dark lump. He stood and began to walk to it, realizing that his powers went missing along with his clothes, when he landed in this desolate landscape. With nothing against which he might gauge distance, walking across the white plane seemed slow and futile, so he started to trot and then to run as fast as his legs would carry him.

Finally, breathlessly, he approached the object of his fascination, fell to his knees, and realized that it was moving. It was a baby. He knew that face from the pictures his mother kept in a frame by her bed!

Adrian stopped and stared at the tiny child lying on his back, smiling, and gurgling with baby sounds. The infant sat up and then stood, as it matured into a toddler wandering around in circles, flapping his arms like an infant bird learning to fly, while singing a lullaby that he heard his mother sing, and continuing to grow.

Within minutes, the child became the mirror image of Adrian and he stared into his own blue eyes with curiosity and wonder. His other self giggled, as he continued to develop into a young man with long blond hair that slowly turned gray. Tiny creases formed around his eyes and mouth but his body remained strong and firm.

He noticed the scars on his right leg, as the other Adrian slowly became an old man, who stooped slightly and moved with some difficulty, favoring his injured limb. A mane of white hair tumbled down his back and a long beard appeared on his wrinkled face. His blue eyes still sparkled but they looked tired, sad, and wise.

"Am I you?" inquired Adrian.

The old man gazed at the boy with a glare that affirmed his impatience with the question, "You already know the answer. I am you as you are me."

Adrian smiled, "So, we live to be old?"

The old *seer* grunted, "Growing old isn't what it's cracked up to be!" He brushed back his hair to reveal scars on his forehead and behind his ear, turned his back to expose more, and lifted battered arms to bare numerous wounds on either side of his chest. "We have paid dearly for the privilege!"

"I would assume that my battles are not finished."

"You've only survived the initiation!"

"Zepallo?" asked the young *seer*.

"And others…as you will learn, the Dark Forces are layered like an onion, as deep as the sea, and more sinister and evil than you might ever imagine. Their tentacles reach into places that will truly astonish you. You'll learn the necessary lessons at Orana's hand but they're merely preparation for all the challenges we face in the future. Even she can't teach you everything that you'll need to know. A lot of it will come to you at the moment when you see the real challenge and the true path to understanding the reality behind the commotion. There are no rules that apply to the things we must do and no one ever gave us a guide book!"

Adrian paused, "Is there joy in our life?"

The old man smiled sadly, "Life is filled with joy and wonder. It's everywhere and in everything. It's in every child's smile, every animal that you will encounter, every day that ends without a battle, and every calm moment that you enjoy. Looking back on it all, I'd say that you should be thankful for every normal day. Days when nothing happens, when you could be bored, when things are confined to everyday routines, those are most precious.

We all take life for granted. New days arrive with every sunrise. Used up days disappear and are replaced. We just assume that this pattern will go on forever and we don't pay enough attention to the little things that are the very reason for our struggles. Take the time to enjoy the most simple moments in life. That's what it's all about."

"I notice a great sadness in your eyes," whispered the young *seer*.

"We've paid a heavy price for our beliefs," replied the old man, quietly.

"Was it worth it?"

The old *seer* pressed a crooked finger to his lips for a moment, as he thought about the question, then burst out laughing, which took a while to ripple through his system, "I honestly don't know the answer to your question. We're not finished yet!"

"You know what I mean!"

"I know, I know. I'll tell you this much, we succeed. Whether the price that we've paid for insuring the survival of the Powers was worth it…yes, I guess it was. There's something else that you must know and that is that you should take the time to really know the people you love and show them how you feel. When you get to be my age, they'll all be gone."

The old man made no attempt conceal the grief in his eyes. Adrian focused on his family, his friends, and all of the people and animals who inhabited his world. He could not imagine outliving all of them, let alone surviving to be this ancient person standing before him.

"How old are you?"

"How old are we?" corrected the elder Adrian. "Well, I guess I'm approaching three-hundred years. We have great-great-great-great-great grandchildren. There are hundreds and I have to confess that I only know a few of them. You'll find two things that inhibit your ability to move about the world. The first is that this body will eventually tire, small wonder after all the punishment we put it through, and the thought of spending time alone becomes more appealing. The second is that we become infamous. Everywhere I go, I'm mobbed by people who want to touch me or to be touched by me. They seem to think that we have some magical power that will save their lives or cure their illnesses or make them rich. We don't."

The young *seer* knew the feeling, as he was always unnerved by the notoriety that resulted from his missions. He could not imagine having to deal with it for the rest of a very long life, "We are shy, aren't we?"

The old man snickered, "That's a nice way to put it. Yes, I still don't like being recognized. The things that we've accomplished had nothing to do with chasing fame or fortune. As you already know, we did it because it was the right thing to do. As you have so often said, 'There is no other choice'."

Adrian nodded, "If there was only one thing that you could tell me, one thing that might help me through the hard parts that lie ahead, what would it be?"

The ancient *seer* sat down on the white ground and crossed his legs, "Listen to your heart, it won't lead you astray. Give love but don't expect it in return. True love is found in the act of giving from your soul and you will know great love in your life."

The old face suddenly crinkled into a mischievous grin, "You already have the love of your life. You just haven't realized it yet but you will."

Adrian was stunned. He was certainly attracted to Morgan. She was beautiful and one of the few people that he felt completely comfortable with...and there was Alius, who was more like a sister and a partner than a girlfriend. He thought about all of the girls and young women in his life and really had no idea who he would choose, if that decision had to be made in this moment.

The old man watched the subtle changes in the expressions on Adrian's face, as he worked through the problem, "Don't waste your time on this, you're a bit young to be considering these things. Just know that, throughout your life, the women hold the key to your happiness and your success...and your survival, for that matter. Love them with all your heart and, when the time comes, the answer to this puzzle will become painfully obvious."

"I'm confused. I thought that Orana said I was going to learn all of the things that I missed as a child?" inquired Adrian, sitting to face his older self.

"All the things that you missed are already inside you. They've always been there and you've been smart enough to follow your instincts, your hunches, that feeling in your gut. You had no reason to develop your talents until you reached Morgan's Knot, because our dear mother neglected to inform us of these wonderful gifts, but we always knew there was something different about us, didn't we?" The old man's face eased into a knowing smile, "You've done well but it will get harder as you go.

I think the lesson that you're supposed to learn from our conversation is that all of those powers course through your system but no one has ever given you any instruction about what to do with the talents that you've already discovered, let alone those you have yet to learn. You just need to let your energy flow out into the world around you. It will move like ripples on a pond, flowing out to touch everything and everyone in your field of focus, and those vibrations will return with information that your senses can interpret.

Our battle with Zepallo is a good example. We knew he couldn't win before the first blow was struck but you also knew that he would survive."

"So, Zepallo is not truly defeated?"

"No, he will rise again and he'll become more powerful and frightening than your last encounter. Those, who held him in check, went down in that submarine our friends destroyed. There's no one to keep him from pursuing his dreams of world domination. He's a wild child sowing seeds of destruction without restraint and there will be none, other than you."

"I guess I knew that when he saluted me, after our battle on the island."

"That salute was his way of saying that you'll duel again. He showed respect for your powers but rest assured, he's not finished with you. There's more to all of this but I'm afraid that we'll have to learn it as time goes by."

Adrian started to protest but the old man smiled and patted him on the knee, "Rules of the game and all that!" He paused to gaze around at the infinite whiteness, "I'm sure the reason that we are having this little chat at the beginning of your instruction is that you must understand that you, and you alone, are the sole sentinel who stands in the way of the Darkness. Certainly, you will have help to win many battles and you'll drive them deeper underground but I'm not sure that we ever actually win the war.

You'll lead the World to long periods of peace and the people and animals will recognize you as a savior. Don't let it go to your head. It means nothing. See your triumphs for what they are...momentary pauses in an ongoing campaign. Enjoy those times...and use them to renew your strength, to expand your talents, and to be with those you love. After all, they are the reason that we do the things we do. You should also know that each battle will demand more of you than the last. As you grow, learn, and develop your strengths, so do your adversaries."

"So, what's the key?"

"The key is something that Master Chi has already revealed to you, 'If you truly believe in the Power of the Light...if you truly believe in yourself, you'll never be defeated.' That's what makes us different, we really do believe."

"Will that belief be tested?"

The old man burst out laughing, "Of course it will be tested! You've already been challenged and you know the feeling we get just before going into battle. Your fear and your doubts will save your life. It is in those moments that you will truly see the course that you must follow, just as you did when you faced Zepallo over the eastern ridge of Morgan's Knot. You knew he couldn't defeat you and your whole being was focused on that evil smile on his face. Everything else disappeared and, in that instant, you both knew that he could not win."

"That was strange. I wasn't really afraid of what might happen because I already knew the outcome in my heart."

"That's it. You knew and you will always know. All of these other things, that you've learned or will come to understand, are inconsequential. They're just tools that you'll develop and use to your advantage. It's our ability to see through the chaos that sets you apart."

Adrian felt a sense of confidence flush through his body. He sat up straight and faced himself.

"Don't get too full of yourself. There will be many times that you'll doubt your own capacity, your judgments, and your powers…and there will be failures and setbacks. Our lifelong depression is debilitating but you'll learn that your escape from that state is accepting the truth…when you truly see, you'll find your focus. There will be times when you'll wish to be just a normal person or that someone else would take on your responsibilities. You already know that you can't be 'normal', you can only follow your path and do your best…and you will pay dearly, in spite of this knowledge."

There was strength and determination in the old man's face but, at the same time, a great sadness. Adrian stared into his old blue eyes and felt that strength flowing between them. He wanted details but knew that this conversation was being presented to guide him through the other lessons that he was about to endure.

"It's strange, but I'm not afraid of facing our enemies. I'm more afraid of losing those who mean the most to us."

"That's as it should be and another reason that you'll find success. You have to defend those who are special to you and, in the process, you'll free the people of the world from the one thing they can't escape, Fear."

"Fear?"

"Yes, Fear…with a capital 'F.' Look around at the world that you're living in…not Morgan's Knot or the Island of the Children…but the real world. What drives everything? Fear! Fear of not having enough or accomplishing enough or not being enough. Fear that someone or some group will come along and take your possessions, your love, or your life. The governments, the religious institutions, and the giant corporations use fear to control, mobilize, and suppress the masses. It's the driving force in this world and you must find a way to put an end to it. Believe me, it's the best thing that we do, although…at the time, we don't realize that our efforts will result in that freedom for everyone else. It just happens."

Adrian was dumbfounded. How could he possibly affect the things that everyone else in the world felt? *That's impossible!*

"I can see that you doubt what I'm saying. Don't. It's a waste of time and energy. Just understand that removing fear is one of the things that we have to accomplish in this battle between Light and Dark. It won't happen because you plan it. It will happen because you'll do what you feel is right and true. It's as simple as that."

"No pressure there!"

"There is no pressure in what I'm telling you. It's simply the truth."

"That's been and will always be the motivation behind the things we do," replied the young *seer*. "Our powers depend on that belief."

"Now you're seeing. Don't get hung up on the eventual outcome or benefits of your efforts. Just do what you must."

"What will you do now?"

The old *seer* paused and reflected on the question, "I don't really know. I'm sure that we're not finished with the things that must be attended to, the times change but hatred and evil still lurk just beneath the surface and rear their ugly heads when we least expect it. I'll admit that I'm getting a bit tired. I've thought that I might move in with Orana and let some of the youngsters take on a more public role but I'm not sure that she would consent."

"Orana's still alive in your time?"

A sly smile crept across his lips, "We're both taking lessons from her, aren't we?"

Young Adrian was speechless. He stammered, "You're taking lessons from Orana?"

"I guess you inspired me to reach a little further and, I have to say, there are some wonderful things that we never dreamed possible...but, then, you have enough to worry about for the moment!"

The boy stared into the old man's eyes. There was so much there and yet, Adrian felt he was hiding parts of it, important parts, perhaps. "When I get to be you, will I be proud of our accomplishments?"

The old man sat up straight and looked directly into the young *seer's* eyes, "Yes, you will be proud...but you'll also be humbled...happy to have known love, sad to have outlived it...proud of the changes that will happen in the world during our lifetime but nostalgic for the...I don't know, innocence and wonder of our initiation into the Powers and the Balance. Maybe that's it, the Balance I mean. Life balances out. There's more good than evil. There's more love than hate. What you put into life is certainly returned many fold but there's always a price to pay for the things that we hold most dear. I'll leave it at that. Let's try to leave the world in balance with itself before we go. Fair enough?"

With a wink, the old *seer* vaporized into a rainbow mist drifting across the plane in a dissipating cloud. Adrian was left alone in the white world to contemplate his future, pondering the question, "And how are we going to do that?"

Chapter 2

Hours, perhaps days, passed, while the boy sat alone on the white plane contemplating the strange introduction. He had so many questions and felt that the conversation seemed exasperatingly incomplete. His mind was working at peak efficiency, trying to file every word, every thought that passed between them, every change in the expression in those blue eyes, every movement or gesture, and every hint that might be buried in the things that were said. He knew himself well enough to know that, had the positions been reversed, he would only reveal the bare minimum but he also knew that he would have phrased his comments so that secrets hidden in the words might become obvious when they were needed.

He struggled with his thoughts, overwhelmed by the brief encounter, and he was still having trouble comprehending the whole, let alone individual phrases.

Finally, he calmed himself and realized that this was just one lesson in his course in the Powers. The experience had not been frightening but it was, certainly, unsettling…knowing that he would live to be a very old man, that he would outlive his friends and family, and that he would eventually succeed in driving the Dark Forces back into the shadows.

His mind settled on the concept of fear. Morgan's Knot provided everything that one might need to live in balance with nature. The sense of security was taken for granted, until he considered the outside world and the troubles that seemed to explode in various locations across the globe in an endless succession of barbarities. Some were certainly internal matters but how many were fermented by the Legio Obscurum? He had no idea but suspected that many of those confrontations were spawned at the command of his foe.

Fear. He had known fear in many forms since arriving on the island, yet he had never been afraid of death, which seemed even farther from his reality, especially after talking with himself, as he would be in the future. No, the fear consuming the present was confined to the two things that touched him on a deeper level…those that he loved and cared for…and the strategy and purpose of his rival.

He felt that he had already found that sense Orana talked about…being able to feel what was happening around him and knowing where the path would lead. His fear was confined to his inability to see beyond that curtain of uncertainty. The most critical point in his studies would demand that he expand his senses to take in everything from every direction, from the past, the present, and the future.

Suddenly, an object tumbled out of the white sky and bounced across the ground to land in front of him. It appeared to be a large pinecone and he started to reach out to pick it up, but it burst into flames. The fire crackled and spit, as each seedpod split and curled back on itself.

The fire dwindled to a smoldering pile of seeds and Adrian leaned over to inspect the remains. One seed sprouted tiny pale roots that burrowed into the white plane. Slowly, a green shoot emerged, writhing and twisting from the seed like a serpent tasting scents on the wind, and began to grow. Within moments, it became a small tree, reaching higher and higher until it touched the white sky. Its girth was now many times his reach and he walked around the base of the huge tree in astonishment that one tiny seed could produce such a magnificent giant. He decided this was a reminder that one of the things he held most dear was his relationship with the natural world. Everything he learned, everything he accomplished had been a result of the power and the example of his animal friends. His own powers were merely an extension of their magic and he was humbled by the realization.

Adrian stared up at the giant tree in awe, "You certainly are a beautiful monster!"

Suddenly, the air fluttered with tiny objects falling across the plain. He reached down and picked up a tiny winged seedpod. "Seeds?"

The seeds began to sprout and plants grew all around him. Trees, shrubs, and flowers clambered across the white plane. The sky turned blue and sunshine filtered down through a canopy of leaves towering above him. A small brook appeared and water gushed over moss-covered rocks and, as he knelt to peer into the little stream, tiny fish struggled against the current.

Birds began to sing and insects buzzed through the foliage. His senses were overwhelmed by the scents, sounds, and colors of the jungle and he was reminded of the beauty of the Island of the Children or the plane of the animals.

In the distance, he heard the roar of a large cat, realizing that this was the world he was destined to protect and nurture. Everything that mattered in his life was centered on that balance.

A parrot flew down and landed on a branch, cocking his head from side to side to inspect the young *seer*. He fluttered his feathers, an iridescent rainbow sparkling in the light.

"You're beautiful!" exclaimed Adrian. "Are you real?"

"Are you real?" squawked the bird. "What's real? Do you believe that you are real?"

Adrian looked down at himself and touched his finger to his belly button. "Yup, I think I'm real…but I'm not so sure about this amazing jungle or the creatures who inhabit it."

"If you believe, then all of this is real. Is the plane of the animals real?"

"Yes, that's very real."

"You're sure?"

"Yes, I'm sure."

"How do you know that it's not just some quirk of your imagination or a dream that seems real…or maybe you're just crazy?"

"Well," smirked the boy, "I don't know that I'm an authority!"

"Well, perhaps I am!" shrieked the bird. "Let's keep it simple for the human, just believe…that's all you have to do…just believe."

"Okay, I believe," laughed Adrian.

"Fine, now shall we go?"

"Where are we going?"

"You're here to learn, are you not?"

"Yes."

"Well, then we should go. You're wasting valuable time!"

The bird flew into the air and landed on Adrian's shoulder, talons digging into his skin, but the boy was so delighted to have someone…or something to talk to, he refrained from complaining.

"Which way shall we go?"

"Why don't you follow the path," suggested his feathered companion sarcastically.

Adrian looked down at the ground and realized that he was standing in the middle of a narrow track winding into the darkness of the forest. He smiled up at the bird and strode out of the sunlight and into the shadows.

As they entered the jungle, he found some large leaves and supple vines and sat down on a large rock to make a loincloth.

The parrot flew to a hefty branch and squawked, "What are you doing?"

"I'm making some clothes. All you birds and animals have beautiful coats. I'm just…pink!"

The gleaming bird cackled and laughed, "Are you embarrassed?"

"Well, no…but humans don't walk around naked. We get to choose our clothing to suit the weather, our moods, or even our sense of style."

"You look fine to me!"

"Well, thank you but I wish I had my robes. They seem to have disappeared when I entered the white world."

"I guess you could have them back," clucked the bird. Adrian looked down at his body, which was suddenly clothed in his blue robes. The young *seer* gazed up at the parrot with a sense of wonder.

"Are you ready now?"

"I'm ready!" exclaimed Adrian. The parrot flew down and landed on his arm. He could hear birds singing, the rustle of leaves in the trees as a gentle wind stirred the air, and animal sounds near and far.

The atmosphere was filled with the sweet scents of the flowers blooming in abundance and his eyes delighted in the electric colors. His senses were so overwhelmed with the wonders of the jungle that he felt secure and comfortable.

The path meandered around giant trees, through dense foliage, and down a small hill to a little stream that flowed with cool water. When he stooped and reached his hand to scoop a handful to sip, the surface erupted in an explosion of movement.

He felt a sting on his hand and jumped back, holding up his arm to find that he was bleeding from several small vicious bites.

The parrot squawked, "You only think that you know the secrets of the natural world. Those little critters are related to the piranha. They could strip all of the meat off a cow in a matter of minutes! Look before you touch!"

Adrian stared up at the colorful bird, as he sucked the blood from his wounds, "I guess I just assume that all of the animals are allies."

"Did you not learn about the creatures of the night? Besides, if you put fresh meat in front of a hungry carnivore, they will eat! It's their nature and they don't care who you are!"

"I see your point," replied the young *seer*, turning back to the path with special care to step on large rocks as he crossed the little stream.

"The point is that you must be aware of everything around you, not just the obvious. You must see with your whole being!"

Adrian was suddenly focused. The warm familiarity and comfort that he felt in the natural world disappeared, replaced with a heightened appreciation for the dangers hiding in his imagined surroundings.

Those animal sounds that seemed so far away, were now located and identified. He knew what creatures were near and far and the direction that each was traveling. A cool breeze was blowing from behind him and the fragrance of the flowers lining the trail left a bitter taste in his mouth. He assumed that the fruit borne of these plants was probably poisonous.

Every sense was primed and ready, although he felt no sense of danger. The parrot on his arm just stared into his eyes, as Adrian stood very still and allowed his senses to explore and define the jungle.

"That's better," squawked the bird, fluttering his rainbow feathers. "I could feel the change in your energies. Now you're ready to proceed."

Adrian focused on the bird, "Do you have a name?"

"Phaschin," replied the parrot.

"Sounds like fashion. Your parents must have known that you'd be beautiful," laughed the *seer*.

"Well, I am beautiful, even a fool like you can see that!"

"I agree. It's just that most of us don't have names that draw attention to the way we look."

"It's not spelled 'fashion'! It's spelled P-H-A-S-C-H-I-N! It's French!"

Adrian laughed, "It is not!"

"Well, it sounds good anyway and, besides, I am beautiful. You said so yourself!"

"Okay, you're beautiful and your name is Phaschin. Are we done with this?"

"Yes," squawked the bird. "You might watch your step. There's a python hanging from the tree up ahead!"

Adrian looked up just in time to duck before coming face to face with a six-foot lime-green python, who was hanging at eye level, flicking his tongue out to sense the identity of the newcomer.

"You're new to the jungle," hissed the snake. "I wonder what you taste like?"

"I'm not your dinner," replied the blond boy. "Besides, I'm much too big and so much would go to waste...or to your neighbors."

"You do have a point but step a little closer and let me taste you. We don't see many like you!"

"Settle down. I'm not impressed," replied the *seer*, leaning against a large bolder that was covered with an electric green moss. "What am I supposed to learn from you?"

The snake stared at him. "If you won't be my next meal, then I guess you should realize that, although all of the animals are willing to join together for the common good, when it's necessary, we all return to our natures after the danger has passed. Just as you have learned about the balance between man and nature, you must understand that there is a balance within nature."

"I'm aware of a hierarchy, or better, a chain from the smallest to the largest and strongest. That is as it has always been and, unfortunately, it's also true in Man. The most powerful prey upon or subjugate the weakest."

"Ah, but you, of all people, should know that your insight is the key to understanding your path along the tightrope between the Dark and the Light. You, meaning Mankind, have a term, an ideal that is different in our world, and that is the concept of justice."

"I understand the word and its meaning."

"Then you must also understand that it's different than revenge. There can be no confusion in your mind. It is your destiny to stand for the Light against the Darkness. Even great leaders of free nations have fallen prey to pride, anger, envy, and greed. The things that you will face are not about you! You're the little Dutch boy with his finger in a dike, holding back a flood of evil chafing to flow across the globe, if you falter."

The snake stared deeply into Adrian's eyes. His tongue flicked, as his head bobbed slowly from side to side. The young *seer* felt that the serpent was trying to hypnotize him, "What's your point?"

"The point is that although you may feel some of those things along the way, you must focus on your true path or you'll become one of them."

"I would never join with Zepallo and his comrades. I've already been through that test!"

"What you have been through, so far, is nothing, compared to what is to come. You must be true to yourself, through every fiber in your body, to the very depths of your soul…or you will fail."

Adrian was quiet, staring back into the prying eyes of the python. He understood what the snake was telling him and honestly believed that he knew the difference between right and wrong.

"What would you do if someone killed your parents or your best friend? Would you allow anger and revenge to guide you?"

"It would be hard to deny those feelings."

"Of course you would react, that's only natural. The question is whether you have enough self-control, enough belief in the Light and the Balance, to follow your path instead of some selfish emotion?"

"I honestly don't know because I haven't been confronted with that nightmare in the short time I've known that I am a *seer*. The only experience that I can relate to what you are saying is when I was asked to replace the balancing crystal on Morgan's Knot. I had just learned the my parents' boat was missing and assumed they were dead."

"Then, perhaps, it's time for some instruction!" hissed the python.

The dark snake slithered across the branch into another tree that was covered with iridescent yellow, orange, and red fruit that resembled peaches. He opened his mouth wide to grab one of the shimmering spheres and brought it back down to Adrian, setting it on the rock beside the young *seer*.

"Here, eat, you must be hungry!" hissed the serpent.

Adrian picked up the fruit and inspected it. The colors glowed deep and rich, and the skin seemed soft. The scent was sweet…almost too sweet, and it was heavy with juice. He was hungry but instead of taking a bite, he placed it back on the rock.

"I think I'll pass, thank you."

"Oh, eat, I know you want it. We all eat this fruit. It's the sweetest in the jungle."

The young *seer* was tempted. His stomach was growling, so he picked it up again and held it up to his open mouth but something seemed odd about the fruit and the temptation being offered. He sniffed the scent and returned it to the rock, "Thank you anyway."

The snake hissed loudly, weaving back and forth, his hypnotic eyes penetrating and searching for the slightest hesitation in Adrian's decision. There was none.

"You have chosen well," hissed the serpent, stretching his body towards the fruit. The glistening orange orb began to decay into a pile of rotten, stinking goo.

"I'm sure there are many parallels in the human world but this simple lesson has been about temptation and about the idea that evil springs from within, not from the outside. It's a potential that each of us carries with us throughout our lives and the true test of your integrity is whether you will succumb to your own fears and desires in the darkest times. That will be the moment when you know who you really are and the stuff from which you are made."

The snake suddenly disappeared in a flash of magenta.

Phaschin, who had been quiet throughout the conversation, squawked loudly, "Evil creature!"

"I didn't hear any protests from you," replied Adrian.

"I'm not here to tell you what to do. My job is to make sure that you follow your path!"

"You didn't want to be eaten," said Adrian, scrambling up a hill.

Chapter 3

The narrow path twisted beneath a tall canopy of trees blocking all but occasional patches of sky. Sunlight streamed through the gaps, cascading through the foliage to reveal the intense colors of flowers or a soft cloud of ferns draping the floor of the jungle.

Occasionally, Phaschin would fly off his shoulder to feed on seeds and nuts growing on shrubs and trees along the passage. Neither had attempted to converse since they left the pile of goo on the rock, which was just as well, because Adrian was concentrating on opening his senses to take in everything around him. He knew there was a wild boar burrowing ahead on the right, near a stream, and a female tiger and her cubs were watching his progress from beneath the drooping canopy of the massive banyan tree growing from a rise to his left. A barred owl perched silently on a tree branch on his right, with a squirming snake in his talons that was not quite dead.

He tried to stretch, to feel the energies of all of the creatures of the forest, to smell their scents, to hear and understand their calls, to track their movements and know their motives. Thus far, he only sensed their curiosity. He understood that he was an intruder in their world, even if he was not quite sure whether any of this was real.

As he approached a stream crossing the path, the wild boar was firmly entrenched on the opposite bank, drinking the cool water. He did not seem ready to give way.

Adrian knelt down on the damp earth, "Is it safe to drink this water?"

The giant black pig just grunted.

Phaschin landed on his shoulder, "I don't think you'll find this one too friendly. We tend to stay out of their way."

Adrian reached up to stroke the rainbow colored bird, "We mean him no harm. Is it safe to drink from this stream?"

"Well, he is, so I guess you can too!"

The young *seer* leaned down and hesitantly reached to scoop up a handful of water. The surface of the water remained calm and the boar grunted again, "If I'm drinking from it, you can too! Do you think I've soiled it or something?"

"Oh, no," replied Adrian. "It has nothing to do with you. I put my hand in another stream and tiny fish tried to tear my skin off!"

"Didn't your mother teach you to look before you touch?"

"Yes, she did."

"Well then, do as she instructed!"

Adrian shook his head, slurping the cool sweet water from the cup of his hand. He had been concentrating so hard on feeling everything around him that his stomach growled, protesting his disregard for nourishment and thirst.

Phaschin squawked, "Now you sound like him!"

"I'm hungry but I have to admit that I'm a bit hesitant about eating any of the fruits that I've seen in the jungle, after seeing what happened to the fruit of the snake."

The boar grunted deep and low, "What are you doing in our forest, if you don't even know which plants provide nourishment and which are poisonous?"

"You have the advantage of knowing the forest. Your parents taught you to eat certain plants and to avoid others, did they not?"

"You are correct but then, you already have all the tools you need. Use your eyes and your nose. Try those red berries on that bush over there and see if you like them."

Adrian stood and walked over the bush, lush with green leaves. The berries looked plump and ripe and they smelled sweet, but there were thorns protruding from every limb on the bush. He pulled his hand up into the sleeve of his robes and pushed it into the bush. Just as he eased his fingers out to grab a cluster of berries, the branches of the shrub snapped around his arm, the thorns tearing his robe and digging into his flesh.

He screamed and frantically pulled with all his might, the bush raking his arm. His sleeve was shredded and his flesh bleeding but he had a handful of berries, which he plopped in his mouth. The flavor was far more rich and savory than anything that he had tasted before and he wanted more.

Looking around the ground, he found a large stick. He barely poked the tip of the staff into the bush before it was entwined in thorns. Pushing the limb to the side revealed a cluster of berries. He plunged his hand in, to grab a handful, and the branches on the other side of the hole enveloped his arm. Pulling his hand inside the remains of his sleeve, he yanked it free. He did not even notice a trickle of blood dripping from his hand, as he plopped one berry after another into his mouth.

He walked around the bush, again and again, looking for the easiest berries to pick. Phaschin commented, "That looks like it might be more trouble than it's worth! Your hand is bleeding!"

"Oh, so it is," replied Adrian absently, as he continued to look for an opening in the bush.

"I'm sure there are other things that we could find to eat."

"But these…berries…aren't like anything that I've ever tasted. They're sweet beyond fresh sugarcane and delicate, like the richest raspberry…only more so! I can't stop eating them. I just have to be intelligent enough to outsmart this bush!"

"I don't think you'll win. So far, your sleeve is in tatters, your hand is a mess, and you've only managed a few berries!"

Adrian's mind was racing, *"I could burn the bush but that would ruin the fruit. If I had an ax I could chop it down…or a shovel, I could dig it up!"* Around and around he walked, in total concentration. Finally, he found another stick and formed a cross, which he pushed down to the top of the bush.

The thorny branches instantly encased his brace revealing several clusters of berries and he leaned in to take them. The bush released the crossed branches and raked his arm and shoulder, as he pulled back, blood running from his cheek, neck, shoulder, lower arm, and hand, as he gobbled his meager prize. He began to pace again.

Phaschin flew down from his perch on a low-hanging limb of a burr oak, landed, digging his talons into Adrian's left shoulder, and whispered in his ear, "I think we should talk."

Adrian reached his bloodied right hand to brush the bird away but the parrot pecked hard on his ear with a sharp beak. "I said, I think we should talk!"

The young *seer* stopped in his tracks and looked up at the bird, who was twisting his head from side to side with an inquisitive and insistent stare. He inspected his hand and the tatters of his sleeve. His face and chin were covered with the juice of the berries and the blood from his scratches, a purple stain dribbled down the front of his blue robes, "What just happened?"

The parrot squawked, "You tell me what just happened!"

"I just wanted more berries…"

"You abandoned everything you know, every power that you possess, and lost all connection with the world around you…let alone wounding yourself, for a handful of berries?"

Adrian was stunned, staring first at his hand and then at the bush, which was showing luscious berries near its surface. He turned back to the bird, "How could I become completely possessed with something so simple that I completely let go of everything that…I am?"

"Pop quiz! What are you supposed to learn from this?"

The *seer* looked down at the moss on the ground and thought about the question. "First, I think that I'm not as focused or mature as I thought I was. Second, I was hungry but that wasn't why I wanted more berries. They certainly taste wonderful but the challenge of possessing them became even more important. I didn't see the bush in its true character and I abandoned everything that I've learned. That's probably what they call an obsession."

"Not to mention gluttony!" smirked the beautiful parrot. "You didn't offer any to me!"

"I should be embarrassed for the way I've acted, especially when you've been kind enough to help me find my way through the jungle."

"Right you are! You should be ashamed!"

"Well, I wouldn't go that far," laughed Adrian.

"What have you learned?"

"I've learned that losing focus is far easier than I might have imagined. I'm not as strong as I thought and I have a lot to learn, before I can become the *seer* everyone seems to expect me to become."

"I think you've got the gist of it, laddy!" replied the parrot. "And remember that gluttony is always punished."

The light was beginning to fade and Adrian yawned and rubbed his stomach, "My tummy hurts and I think it's time for a little rest. Give me a few minutes and then we'll continue with our journey."

With that, he sat down on the soft moss on the ground, curled into a ball, and fell fast asleep.

~

As Adrian drifted off, his mother's voice called from a distance. He was standing on a craggy hill staring into a squatty molten blob of orange melting into the horizon. The forbidding shadows of the jungle crept around the rocky cone and offered no counsel, so he opened his senses and searched for the direction of the sound.

Again, his mother's voice called slowly, softly, "A...d...r...i...a...n..."

He focused on a clump of trees to the north and started running down the steep hill. Loose rocks slipped underfoot and he started sliding, falling over backwards, tumbling in an avalanche of jagged stones to the bottom. Spreading his arms and legs to break the roll, he slid on this back until a thicket of brambles absorbed him unceremoniously.

Rubbing his right arm and hand, he tore his other sleeve extricating himself from the thorny brush and felt blood dripping from the abrasions on his back.

Again, the call, "A…d…r…i…a…n…"

The boy darted into the shadows beneath a dense thicket of palm trees and peered into the darkness of the dense jungle. He crouched low in a curtain of tall grass, allowed his eyes to adjust, and waited for his mother's voice. There were no birds singing, although he could hear water running over rocks, a short distance into the forest, and the wind whistling through the trees. In fact, he could not hear any living creatures. He released a long slow sigh and felt for the energies around him, nothing was moving. The pulsing vitality of life that radiated through the jungle was replaced by an eerie stillness.

His mother called again and he charged through the underbrush, into a grove of tall slender bamboo towering like a great green picket fence reaching up through a sunlit gap between the giant trees. Focused on the direction of her voice, he came upon a large rock formation growing out of the floor of the forest, jutting straight up like the petrified trunk of the granddaddy of all trees. It appeared that the stones had been shattered by some gargantuan power and jammed together into this giant black obelisk.

He walked around the base of the rock until he found a smooth upright stone that resembled a door. In the center, he found a keyhole. Reaching into the pocket of his robes, he withdrew his golden key and inserted it into the slot. The rock cracked down the center and hinged open, revealing a path winding into a dark void. He stepped through the threshold and the boulder rumbled closed behind him.

He called out, "Mother! Are you there?"

"I'm here, darling," responded his mother's voice. "Come to me, I have a surprise for you!"

Adrian stumbled through the dank boggy decay, over slimy tree trunks fallen haphazardly across the forest floor, until he saw a dim shimmer in the distance. He clamored straight to it until his mother's face appeared slightly behind the glare of the light, as though he was searching for features through a gauzy curtain in a sunlit window.

That excruciating jolt raced up his spine, exploding at the base of his skull, as he stepped into the halo of the glow. Someone else was standing behind his mother and it was not his father. The figure was tall and powerful, dressed in a dark cloak, and his hands caressed his mother's shoulders. It was Zepallo!

He reached into his pocket to retrieve the ring that Dadeus had given him when he, Alius, and Raffe traveled across the globe to connect all the nodes and aimed at the Dark Lord's wicked smile.

His mother moved between them and held up her hand, "Stop. There will be no violence today."

Adrian lowered his ring, "I don't understand."

Sara smiled, stepped forward, and reached to embrace her son, "There are many things in life that we can't accept, until we have time to understand their true significance."

"What do you mean?"

"There's another side to this man that I've grown to love and you will too, if you give him a chance."

"You know that will never happen!" shouted the boy.

"Adrian, calm down. There's nothing to be upset about."

"What about Dad?"

"Oh, he understands that things in life change, that blood is thicker than water. He gave us his blessing."

"I'm sorry but I can't believe that."

"But you must, because it's true!"

Adrian crumpled to his knees. "This can't be happening. You talk of love when you know that his heart is as black as night. You've seen his evil, his complete contempt for life."

"I only see his power!" laughed his mother, as she turned and looked lovingly into Zepallo's eyes. "If you join us, we can be the future of the world!"

"That's a world you raised me to fight against. That future is shrouded in darkness."

"Aren't you tired of fighting? Don't you wish that we could find an accommodation that might settle everything, once and for all? Your future could be filled with all the power and riches that dreams are made of…only this future could be real!"

"I have no use for power or riches. The riches I hold most dear are my love for you, for our family and all of our friends, for the animals and the beauty of nature, and the joy and the promise of the Light. That's what I stand for and that's what I am!"

"Just give us a few days to convince you. I promise that you'll agree, if only you'll give it a chance." His mother smiled her most endearing smile, as she knelt down to lean close to his face. "Love, like the love I feel, touches us so rarely in a lifetime and it must be a miracle when fleeting love lost is found. I want to share it with you."

"Mother, you know I can't agree to this. I can't allow this. I would be fighting against the person who is most dear to me, you…and you're the reason that I've fought so hard, taken so many chances, and risked my life. You're the light in my life, the shining example of all that is good in our world…but one of us will not survive this."

"If that's your choice, then so be it!" shrieked his mother, with a fierceness that he had never witnessed before. "I've chosen my future!"

"Mother, you can't! I won't let you!"

"What are you going to do, kill me? Or kill Zepallo? He's far stronger than you'll ever be, you'd not last a minute. No, my son, you must make a choice between your immature efforts to fight for the fading Light or the promise of our family unified and determined. It's as simple as that. Make a choice," screamed Sara, standing at Zepallo's side, wrapping her arms around his waist, and smiling up into his cold blue eyes.

Adrian felt his heart twisting in his chest. The pain of the injuries he suffered in his battles could not compare to the agony that tore through his entire being. A dark shadow rolled across everything that was most precious in his life…his belief in the Powers, in the animals, in the most basic concept of the Darkness and the Light, in the goodness and fulfillment that life within the Balance provided, and in his own family...his own mother!

For the first time, since embarking on this journey, he doubted. He doubted himself. He was not sure that his own powers were sufficient or his dedication to his path and his mission was worth losing the one person who represented everything he believed in his soul. Was it possible to continue this war without the spirit of his mother to guide and inspire him?

The words, of his older self, echoed through his mind, *"We have paid a heavy price for our beliefs."* He realized that, sooner or later, all of his family and friends would die but that expectation was far easier to absorb and accept than his own mother joining Zepallo. That was a price too dear.

The Dark Lord's voice was deep and powerful, although it lacked the venom that Adrian felt in their past encounters. "It seems to me that you have several options here. First, you could join with your mother and me to free the population of the world. Nothing could stop us and the rewards would be unending! The second possibility is that you could try to kill one or both of us and, we both know, that you don't really want to kill your dear mother. Firing a blast at me would be foolish at best. The third is that you can choose to die. It's up to you."

"You know I could never join you and we both know I defeated you the last time we met. You have power and experience. I have youth, energy, speed, creativity, and my belief in the Power of the Light. Are you willing to risk a duel?"

Zepallo held Sara close and withdrew a long black crystalline saber from a sheath on his belt. He extended the blade to touch the glowing tip to the young *seer's* nose. "Does this mean that you have chosen to die?"

He suddenly felt the assurance, the confidence that filled his heart during their battle over Morgan's Knot, drain from his body. The realization that he might die in this moment frightened him but there could be no retreat. To show any fear, to pull back...even subconsciously, would determine the balance in any future confrontations.

Adrian raised his ring in defense but he knew that he could not get a clean shot at his enemy without injuring his mother. The two warriors stood motionless, staring into each other's eyes, the black sword touching the very tip of Adrian's nose while he aimed his ring at Zepallo and his mother.

He tried to levitate, for a better angle, but his missing powers sapped his confidence, leaving him defenseless and confused. The confrontation had evolved into a stalemate. The young *seer* could not retreat, he could not rise to the challenge that Zepallo presented, and he was not ready to die. How could this be happening?

He raised his hands in the air, tipped his head back, and let out a roar, "Mother don't do this! Come back to me!"

Thrashing wildly, he opened his eyes to find Phaschin sitting on his chest, pecking at his nose trying to wake him. "That must have been an awful dream!"

"Dream? Are you sure it was a dream?" gasped Adrian, struggling to sit up. The jungle was dark and quiet. An owl called in the distance, a dove cooed softly in a tree behind him, and a very large cat was snoring less than twenty yards up the path. His senses had returned and he opened himself to the glow of everything in the forest.

"You've been asleep for quiet some time," replied the parrot. His head bobbed from side to side and his dark eyes glistened with his concern. "Then you started rolling around on the ground, screaming for your mother and yelling at someone else, but I couldn't make out who that was."

"It was a dream," whispered Adrian. Tears rolled down his cheeks and his chest heaved, as he gasped for air. "I think I'm beginning to understand."

"Understand what?" inquired the beautiful bird, cocking his head. The iridescent colors of his feathers glimmered in the shafts of moonlight dripping down through the dark canopy of giant trees towering above them.

It took a few moments for Adrian to calm himself, "My weaknesses, the holes in my powers, they're all tied to my love for my people and the beliefs that I've fought so hard to protect. Love is the hole in my armor and, at the same time, the reason that I must continue!"

"Well, it's nice that you've got that all figured out. You scared me to death. I thought you were dying or something…worse!"

"No, no…don't you see? It's all about love. Love is the reason that we go out and fight the battles that we must, while it's also the soft spot in our hearts that makes us vulnerable. I think I see what I was saying."

"Now you're really making sense!" squawked the bird in frustration.

"Before I met you, I had a conversation with myself…only my other self was about three hundred years old and knew everything that I want to know now. He told me there would be a great price to pay for the things that I'll accomplish in my lifetime. The great price has to do with the love I feel and my inability to control it. Love isn't something you just go out and find. It comes to you, infects you, and fills you with everything that's good in the world. It isn't something you instruct yourself to feel, it just happens, and with the joy that love brings, there's also heartbreak and sorrow. One can't exist without the other. That's the price we must pay for the privilege of feeling these things."

"I wish I knew what you're talking about!"

"Oh, never mind. The point is…I understand," said Adrian, as he stood up and brushed moss and leaves from his tattered robes. "Are you ready to go?"

"Where are we going?"

"Wherever the path leads. There are more lessons to be learned and I'm ready to begin!"

Before Phaschin could respond, the jungle melted away, replaced with the white plain, the white sky, and nothingness. Adrian sighed and sat down on the ground, alone with his thoughts.

~

A low rumble, quaking through the mantle beneath his trembling body, interrupted the quiet emptiness of the white plain and, instinctively, he tried to levitate into the air.

A giant rock exploded through the white ground, swelling into a small mountain, which groaned into a big mountain, and then a mountain range. Frightened by the roar of stone grating against gargantuan stone, Adrian kept climbing higher, striving to concentrate, to remain calm and focused through the din and the thunderous upheaval. Suddenly, there was silence and he felt tiny and vulnerable, surrounded by enormous craggy rocks soaring into the sky.

Clouds formed and tumbled over the precipice, filling valleys with curtains of moisture, ghostly white vapors dancing in a gusty breeze. Adrian looked up into the stormy sky and a single drop of rain landed on his nose, splattering across his face, the first followed by another, then another, loosing a deluge from giant thunderheads. Lightning flashed and thunder rolled across the heavens, as bloated clouds billowed to shroud the horizons.

The young *seer* pulled up the cowl of his robes and took refuge beneath an outcropping of rock that promised shelter, pressing a shivering body against cold stone to watch the rain drip into tiny pools that joined together forming little streams that flowed into larger torrents that tumbled down the mountain.

Without warning, the rock beneath his feet gave way, with a mighty crack, and he tumbled into a small river that swept him into a raging current. His body bounced along the rocky bottom, then released to the surface. He gasped for breath and attempted to levitate out of the rapids but he could not harness his powers. Harboring no doubts that he was at the mercy of the elements, the desperate *seer* tried to dodge the large boulders erupting in his path and avoid the swirling eddies in their wake.

The small tributary was joined by other streams, merging into a large river coursing down through a steep valley, clawing its way through miles of jagged formations. In the distance, a loud roar echoed up the canyon and the flow propelled him, a soggy cork crashing towards the blind precipice with no escape.

Sputtering, he bobbed to the surface and tumbled down a wash, where the valley spilled into a broad gorge. He spied a line of raging waves, linking the rock walls on either side of the torrent, and doom lurking in a dark stormy sky visible beyond the breakers.

He struggled to turn his feet downstream, as he rushed through a boulder field at the head of the giant waterfall. A churning whirlpool dragged his ragged body through a gravel bed before catapulting him out into mist spewing a billowing steamy veil across the cascade. He fell for hundreds of feet and, just before smashing into the rocks at the bottom, managed to recover enough control to levitate into the vapors.

He spun around to view the waterfall and was awestruck by its height and breadth. Enormous flows, more than a thousand feet wide and broken by rocky protrusions, green with gnarly little trees, moss, and ferns, fired off the top, eternal white columns dropping into the canyon below. The roar was overwhelming, the air reverberated with endless concussions, and brilliant rainbows danced through the mist.

At the bottom, the crashing falls and tumbling rapids merged into a broad slow river ambling through knobby foothills that spilled into a great empty expanse. Adrian soared along its course through rocky narrows and broad flats, increasing his speed until he reached the edge of an endless expanse, where the ruddy floodwaters rushed out across the featureless plain in a magnificent blue wave that rolled into the horizon.

The young *seer* hovered just above the crest, almost surfing on the mightiest wave in the world, and rolled to watch the curve of the horizon swallow the mountains, until the highest peak dropped into an infant ocean, spilling in every direction to cover the planet.

His power of levitation faltered and he made a vain attempt to molt into an eagle but, thrashing wildly, he crashed into the massive surge consuming the white plain. The force of the undercurrent pulled him into the depths of the ocean and, for a moment, he convulsed in panic as his last breath expired and water rushed through his nose and mouth to fill his lungs. He was certain that he was about to die, until he remembered Dadeus immersing him in the tank on the Island of the Children.

Hesitantly, he tried to inhale and found that he could breath. The clear water seemed pure and clean and full of oxygen. He could see for a long distance and realized that, other than clouds of chalk and sand churning up from the bottom, there was nothing in the water. There was no life, no bits of seaweed or kelp, no fish, no corrals, nothing living on the ocean floor, for this was the sea as it was in the beginning…violent, cold, and empty.

As the currents carried him deeper, he spied formations of rock jutting from the sand on the floor of the sea. Black clouds erupted and bubbled to the surface far above him. He swam near one of the vents and noticed tiny yellow bumps on a gray funnel spewing the dark gases. Curious, he swam closer to inspect this strange and beautiful collection of oval shapes, in spite of shimmering heat boiling up around the spout, glistening in what little light filtered down to this depth.

The tiny yellow polyps growing from just beneath the mouth of the vent, down the rocks to the sandy bottom, reacted when he reached to feel their texture. A few spongy yellow splotches stuck to his fingers and they were moving! Could this be the place where life began? He inspected the tiny yellow blob in wonder. The tiny cells floated away and soon the water was filled with clouds of miniature creatures scurrying in every direction.

The progression rushed forward with tiny cells consumed by larger creatures, which were devoured by even larger forms, and those were eventually inhaled by something that resembled a primitive fish. Kelp and sea grasses sprouted from the bottom and corrals bloomed into elegant fluid colonies, providing homes for many other species. Large crab emerged from craggy shelters and scrambled across the sand, searching for a meal while avoiding predators. Adrian felt compelled to follow, as they raced ahead on eight legs and noticed that the bottom was sloping up, reaching to touch the air. Light streamed down through the darkness, electric fingers stabbing, flashing, and dragging him to the surface.

Adrian exploded from the murky water into glorious sunshine and rode a massive wave through the surf to clamor onto a beach, where he collapsed, sprawling on the sand and retching the water clogging his lungs. He gasped for fresh air and delighted in the warmth and the scent of the salty breeze.

He rolled onto his back and realized that the dunes above the beach were covered with windswept grasses clinging tenaciously to the sandy soil and beyond the ridge, he could see a forest of pine trees standing straight and tall against a bright blue sky. A seagull swooped low, investigating this strange creature, cawing his displeasure when Adrian moved, rising to watch a cloud float across the sky, thankful to be alive and humbled by the power of the natural world.

$\sim$

Adrian tried to settle into that calm quiet, where his mind was free to roam, to explore things hidden at the very core of his heart.

He inhaled slowly, deeply, and willed every muscle to relax. Thoughts and feelings began to flow from his subconscious with no particular order in their appearances, although it felt as if he was watching all the extra bits of life in a rather strange stilted film flickering inside his mind.

Love was the reason for everything. He saw his parents, Elsie and George, the twins, the Professor and Ester, Morgan, Alius, Raffe, little Kelly, Josh, Ian, Sammy, Sky, Master Chi and countless others…each held a special place inside his heart, for each in their own way represented the best of our species. Certainly, we all bear frailties and weaknesses, they are the work of life, but the people who passed through his mind possessed unique and wonderful qualities that touched those around them with intelligence, bravery, kindness, and compassion.

His vision expanded to include the *seers,* the Keepers, and all of the animals, and then settled on the vibrant beauty of life inhabiting every nook and cranny across the Earth. It provided the spark that allowed life to evolve and expand and without the continuing generosity of Mother Earth, we would certainly perish. Yet, Man has consumed the bounty and the riches of the Earth for thousands of years, without giving much thought to the idea that perhaps, someday, we will have used it all up.

In a flash of inspiration, he realized that his responsibility extended beyond defending the Balance and the Powers, beyond his family and friends, beyond the animals…if he was to lead the battle of the Light against the Dark, then he would have to defend the physical planet, the place that we all call home.

Every living thing deserves clean air and water, a safe place to live and grow, renewable foods and resources, and the promise of hope for the future of their children and grand-children.

His vision zoomed out to the entire globe…the oceans, rivers, mountains, forests, plains, deserts, cities, villages, islands, and everything that lived on, above, or beneath the surface of the Earth. The blue jewel in his mind glowed with a golden energy pulsing with life, a shared spark coursing through our bodies and bound to the universe that surrounds us. Everything and everyone is connected on the most basic level, created and composed of the same atoms and molecules that make up the Earth, the seas, and the sky.

Finding a way to protect it all seemed daunting and unrealistic but he could not see this vision in small pieces. Every facet was bordered by others demanding inclusion and, as his mind explored the possibilities, he realized that leading the Light against the Dark had more to do with our continued existence on this planet, rather than the glory of winning a definitive battle against an enemy. A realization that made him feel very small and humble.

If he was truly chosen to lead, then he would have to learn to reach the masses, to make them understand the stakes in a war that has been raging secretly for centuries. It was one thing to lead his fellow *seers* and the animals against an evil army and quite another to allow himself to become known throughout the world, to give up the secure quiet life on Morgan's Knot, while exposing the secrets that had been held in safekeeping for thousands of years, and, finally…painfully, to get past his secret fear of being viewed as different or being excluded by normal people, who did not possess these strange and wonderful powers.

He thought about the trip back from the Island of the Children, when Morgan found him crying in the bow of the Jasmine. He was worried about living up to everyone's expectations, of not being just one of the kids, and she reminded him that he could not revert to being the child that he was when he arrived on the island.

He smiled to himself, as he heard her words inside his head. She was right. She was always right and the thought applied to this problem. It always seemed to come down to the idea that there really is no choice, other than to do what you know you must. This was no different, although it did make him uncomfortable to think that he would have to stand before millions, if he was ever going to convince them of the life that's possible and the threat that lies just beneath the surface, conspiring to cast a long shadow across the planet.

The only way the Dark Forces could be defeated, once and for all, was for everyone on the planet to join together, to rise up to confront the danger of the Darkness. To reach that goal, everyone would have to overcome the one thing that we all share…fear.

He heard the voice of his older self, "Fear with a capitol 'F'!" and he recognized that he was beginning to understand what that statement really meant. There is nothing to fear, when we all join together for the common good. The promise of tomorrow is not about politics or economics, religion or spiritual beliefs. It is about working together to care for our world and for each other, if there is any hope for survival.

He wondered, *"Could it be that simple? Could the future of the world be determined by making people accept one rather obvious thought as truth? That would be too easy. Well, not easy but…?"*

Adrian was roused from his meditation by a low murmur that sounded like an approaching cloud of bees swarming around him. He opened his eyes to find a ring of people and animals, all humming different tones and staring down at him. He levitated just above their heads and realized that there were thousands, perhaps, millions stretching as far as his eyes could see across the plain. Slowly, he turned around and around, amazed at the incredible diversity in the crowd. Certainly, there was every animal, attending in astonishing numbers, and people of every description…tall people, short people, thin people, fat people, fair people, dark people, those from the north and the south, the east and the west…there was no group not represented.

Slowly they began to chant, "We've been waiting for you! Our future, your future, and the future of the world, depends on you!"

Adrian bowed his head with respect and the very real sense that he was humbled by their demand and their trust. The insecurities that he harbored about his ability and his responsibility to become a spokesman for the world, suddenly vanished, replaced by a sense of mission…an understanding that, if he was not yet capable, he would have to work that much harder to gain the tools that might allow him to be all that these creatures and people expected of him. To strive to be any less would guarantee disaster and defeat. The vision of his true path suddenly became clear and focused.

His older self appeared in the crowd, dressed in blue robes, waving to the young *seer*, "We certainly don't know how to learn things the easy way, do we? We should have got this one without all this…help." He gestured to the thousands encircling them, "Don't ya' think?"

Before Adrian could reply, the image faded, the crowd disappeared and he was left hovering, alone above the white plain.

Chapter 4

As the boy pondered the most secret fears that he would have to overcome, a large leather-bound book fell out of the sky, crashing onto the smooth white plain directly in front of him with an enormous 'Thud!' The heavy binding of the ancient book was tattered but the title, though faded, read 'The End of Times'. Beneath the crackled guilt lettering, where an author's name might appear, was a single word, 'Everyman'.

He knelt before the massive tome and heaved the cover open but the stained and yellowed pages were blank, as he flipped from front to back, except the last page, which read, "The End."

Adrian stared at the words and wondered what he was supposed to learn from this enormous book with no words between its covers…no instructions, no magical insights?

The sky darkened and stars appeared, millions of flaming arrows streaking through the heavens. Ahead, a single star grew closer, brighter. He could see that it was orbited by planets and the third one was blue. The field of view shifted to follow the progress of a large asteroid, jostled from its orbit in the far reaches of the solar system by the gravity of Jupiter, being drawn into the sun at an astonishing speed.

The giant chunk of rock dipped close to the roiling surface of the star, spun around in a tight orbit, and flew back into space, a shot from a sling, rushing to intercept the Earth. The asteroid took aim at the Pacific Ocean, glowing and sparking, the surface melting and fragmenting into a long fiery tail flailing for thousands of miles, as it burrowed through the friction of the atmosphere and exploded with the force of millions of tons of manmade explosives, just before it reached the surface. An enormous cloud of rocks, ash, and vapors rose up into the atmosphere to be carried by the wind until it completely enveloped the planet, blocking all sunlight and any hope of life.

The scene expanded to the entire Pacific Ocean with volcanoes erupting in the Philippines, Japan, Alaska, off the coast of Seattle, San Francisco, Los Angles, and the southern coast of Mexico like a chain of firecrackers. The displacement of the landmasses churned the seas into tsunamis racing out in concentric rings to smash across the land, erasing everything in their path.

Giant storms grew from the ash spewed from the volcanoes and acid rain fell in torrents washing over every corner of the globe. No plant could survive the onslaught and, again, life ceased to exist.

Another scene revealed patches of Earth that were parched and dry. Drought spread across the richest farmland in the world, populations scattered like swarms of ants scurrying to find fresh water and fertile soil, and starvation proved a slow torturous end for mankind.

The scene changed again and again, this time showing man's inhumanity to man. One clan rising up to slaughter another, the greed of the mighty and powerful at the cost of starvation and suffering for the masses, economic wars fought under the guise of religion…human rights, hopes, and aspirations sacrificed in the name of progress or stolen in the rush to defend individual nations or corporate fortunes. Zepallo's projections, which appeared to Adrian during his capture by the Dark Lord, seemed tame by comparison.

Bombs exploded in great mushroom clouds over the capitols of every nation. Within a few days, without communication or coordination, civilization disintegrated into small tribes of desperate nomads who would stop at nothing to survive. Anarchy replaced law and order. People ran aimlessly in panic, frantic for a way out of the nightmare, to save their lives without concern for anyone else. The strong and powerful took what they needed and killed the weak, civilization's pinnacle of peace and civility long forgotten.

Adrian suffered through rapid-fire scenes of every possible end to life on the planet that he felt fated to protect. He was so overwhelmed by the incredible variety of ways man could cease to exist that he fell over backwards, sprawled on the white plain, staring up into a sky exploding with visions, screaming for the death and destruction to stop.

Orana's voice appeared from nowhere and everywhere around him, "I take it you might have a question."

Adrian gasped for breath, "Which of these horrific images is really the end of the Earth? What am I supposed to learn from a book with no words?"

"This is the final volume. There have been many before it and the pages of those books are filled with the darkest chapters of human history. I'm sure that you're familiar with many of the stories that have been recounted as myths or legends through countless generations. The Forces of Darkness have been busy."

"Am I to understand that when this book is finished, the World, as we know it, will end?"

"I believe that you are correct."

"But who is to write these final chapters?"

"I'm sure that you'll be mentioned but the words, that describe the events that will lead to the end of times, will be written by all of mankind. It is not up to one person but rather all of us."

"Does this mean that we're doomed?"

"No," replied Orana's soft and reassuring voice. "The point is that our actions will determine the final chapters. It could be a very short time or we could continue for many generations. It is entirely up to us."

"I've witnessed Zepallo's version of the apocalypse and it was truly terrifying. The earth was a smoldering ember, the cities destroyed, good people joined with the Dark Forces, abandoning their children along the side of the road, and I could see no hope for the future. Now I've seen almost endless possibilities of natural and manmade disasters that could lead to the end of times."

"That was his version and what you have seen only demonstrates that there are infinite ways that we could all die by natural causes over which we have no control," said Orana in soothing tones.

"We humans can only control what mankind does to this planet and to our future. I believe the point is that it's not up to one person. It's a matter of choice for each and every one of us. The future isn't predestined, as you have learned from your studies of the Books and the Powers. Their interpretation is based on the information that's available at the moment. There are reasons to fear for our future and there are also reasons to hope that we might find our way through the darkness to the light. That's up to you, to me, to all of us."

"My last lesson was about the idea that everything is tied together in a balance that allows life to thrive on our planet. The earth itself is a living organism and we exist, as parasites, only because we have yet to destroy it. I came to the conclusion that my destiny is not only to fight to protect the Balance, but also to protect the physical world. Am I correct?"

Orana laughed softly, "Yes, you've got the concept. Mankind has pillaged the riches of the Earth for thousands of years. At some point, it stands to reason that we'll have consumed the last of her resources, sullied the beauty and wonder, and left nothing for coming generations. Something has to change in the very near future or we will certainly perish by our own greed."

Adrian smiled to himself. He might be young and, in many ways, still immature but he had grasped the correct lesson and taken it to heart. He understood the result he had to strive for, even if he had no idea of how he was going to find the path that would lead him there.

"You are a unique case and the lessons that you are learning were devised for the path that we hope you will follow. Each of us must overcome the demons that live inside, before we can venture out to fight the battles that lie ahead. You must understand the past to see into the future. To triumph in battle, only to fall victim to your own weaknesses, would be a terrible contradiction. As this book demonstrates, the stories of the future have yet to be written. Are you still afraid?"

Adrian pondered the question before responding, "Afraid? No, I think I'm beginning to see beyond my inner fears but I'm also becoming more aware of my vulnerabilities. My strength is the same as my soft spot...my love for those who are most dear to me and my belief in the Powers." He grinned, "I have no interest in wealth or fame, yet I've seen that I'll have to accept whatever lies ahead and learn to use it for the right purposes. Perhaps, rather than shunning these mysteries, I should learn about them, so they might become tools or, at least, offer a better understanding of why they're so important to other people."

"You're beginning to see, to understand a bit of human nature. We're weak creatures, intelligent but often misguided, bold yet afraid, self-centered yet dependent on the rest of the human race, and, certainly, each of us strives for significance while trying to be one of the crowd. You have a bit of that in you."

Adrian laughed, remembering Morgan's words, "It's funny you should mention that because I just revisited that lesson. It's one I'll never forget."

"You wanted to be like everyone else, except you found out that you aren't like everyone else. You're unique, but, then, so is each soul that you will encounter throughout your journey."

"I see your point," laughed Adrian.

"There was no way to tell you that the lessons you must learn are all about the person that you are inside. You already have faith, strength, bravery, and a wonderful sense of right and wrong. No, this is about the inner you. There are plenty of enemies out there ready to wield impressive weapons against you, I can't supply you with anything that you don't already possess or can't learn. You're too young to become a Master *Seer* but what I can teach you is to believe in yourself, to be aware of everything around you...any tiny change in the Balance, and to follow the path you see before you without hesitation. Wisdom will come with experience," laughed the old *seer*. "Usually bad or painful experiences!"

"May I be the first to say that I'm not looking forward to the path to wisdom?"

"It's part of living a real life. As you're learning, the joys come at the cost of the pain that we must endure. There can't be one without the other or we wouldn't have anything to compare."

Adrian smiled, "In other words, if everything was wonderful all the time, we'd probably get bored and look for something…I don't know…bigger, better, or more intense?"

"Precisely!" laughed Orana's voice. "Would we treasure love, if we had never suffered disappointment or loneliness or missing someone who is important in our lives? I think not. Sometimes, we have to lose something that we hold dear to our hearts, just to know how precious it really was!"

"Are you saying we have to lose love to understand how important it was before we lost it?"

"Well, sort of…we all become complacent, accepting whatever standard or level of existence that comprises our lives in the present. Too often we accept whatever is, instead of looking into the future at what might be."

"So, the present is what we make of it?"

"Even more so…the future. This book is full of pages waiting to be filled with the history that you are going to live. It will tell of the triumphs and the defeats, the challenges and the solutions…and, in some cases, the failures, as well as the progression of the human experience…the human awareness of this wonderful world we live in. Is it the End of Days? I don't know and neither do you. You must not only lead the people of the world but convince them to follow, to understand, and to take action to protect all that they've taken for granted for so long."

Adrian looked down at the immense volume sitting like a ragged rock on the white plain. A strong breeze ruffled the pages and butterflies of every color imaginable emerged to flutter into the air…hundreds, thousands, millions glimmering and shimmering all around him. Suddenly, the white world melted away, replaced with the form of Orana sitting in front of the fire on the floor of the cave, smiling at the young *seer.* A bright yellow butterfly flew from her gnarled finger, flitting around the fire and darting to the mouth of the cave.

"I could drill you on levitation, or moving through the vectors or the planes, or improving your skills with weapons…but I won't. Those are things that you can learn from others, my task is to teach you to be strong within yourself, to feel the world around you, and to be brave enough…sure enough to follow your path. Everything else will come as it must."

Adrian peered into her old eyes for the strength, the wisdom that made him feel safe and warm, "I guess I was expecting to fight dragons or something!"

"Don't be disappointed. You're already a brave warrior. The question is whether you'll become a wise leader, one able to detach himself from outside influences and listen to that inner voice." She paused, "It will never misguide you."

"I've learned to trust that voice, although there have been times when I wish it would speak sooner or louder!"

"I know just what you mean. In those times, take heart that you are learning, growing your understanding, not only of your foes but also of the world of the Light. It took many years before I understood that simple idea. I hope that you'll have the advantage of understanding it in your youth. You can't defeat the Forces of Darkness by yourself. You'll need help from the animal world, from your fellow *seers,* and from the Keepers, but you'll also need the help of the common people, those billions living everyday lives with no idea of what's going on just beyond their view…let alone, their responsibility to defend their world. The things that you'll face will force you to reach, beyond the strengths you already know you possess, into a well of inner power and assurance that will see you through your chosen path. You found it when you faced the Dark Lord over Morgan's Knot.

There are two thoughts that you should carry with you. First, no one…and I honestly mean no one, understands the responsibility for which you and I have volunteered. I understand because I've lived these many years and led the good fight through the centuries. You will understand because your path is predestined…you'll take on your enemies because, as you say, there is no other choice."

"That's a phrase that will come back to haunt me!" laughed the young *seer*.

"Little do you know!" giggled the old woman. "The second thing that you should consider is that it's time for you to go. There are disturbances in the Balance and I'm too old to go out to investigate what's happening. Certainly, that scoundrel Zepallo is involved and we both know what that means."

Adrian's smile faded, "How do you know?"

"I feel it, my young charge, and, if you would allow yourself, you'd feel it too."

The blond *seer* closed his eyes and searched for that calm state that he first learned from Simian. His senses took in everything inside the cave and then expanded out into the world. Somehow, he knew that it was a warm dark night outside, the stars were shining and a crescent moon had yet to appear. Beyond the plane of the animals and into the world of the humans, he felt a cold chill run up his spine. There was an emptiness in the texture of his world, he had no idea of what but something had changed and knew he had to hurry, because, in his absence, something was terribly wrong.

He opened his eyes and found Orana staring at him, with a slight smile crinkling the corners of her eyes, "I've been feeling this disturbance since last night but I couldn't interrupt your instruction. Although there are several more scenarios that I would like you to visit, I believe it is time for you to go."

Adrian stood and walked around the fire, kneeling to give his Master a hug and a kiss on her cheek, "Thank you for taking the time to guide me through my lessons. I'll come back to visit you, when I know what's happening out there."

"There's still much for you to learn but, in the meantime, know that I'll be here to listen and to advise but it's up to you to right the wrongs in the world. I'm too old to lead another charge!"

"I'll do my best," smiled Adrian, as he closed his eyes and concentrated. A moment later, he was gone.

Chapter 5

His mind was spinning with the rush of experiences over the past…however long it had been. Each lesson offered insights into his own weaknesses and insecurities, which still made him wonder whether he really possessed the strength or bravery to stand against the many ways that mankind could find to destroy the world, let alone make them understand. That was the key…making them understand and he knew it would take a while before he would see that path clearly, if only because his foray through the white world transformed his entire perspective.

Before he started with Orana's lessons, he believed that he would be learning to fight external enemies but, instead, they taught him that the most fearsome demons exist inside each of us. Learning to control and, perhaps, use that energy for some good purpose seemed life's ultimate objective. He secretly dreamed of the joy of victory when he completed his tasks, yet he felt no elation or relief at having survived to fight another day. Instead, the responsibility, that he first assumed when he climbed the mountain on Morgan's Knot, had grown larger…heavier…and more personal. Even though he was still a boy, the battle for the Powers forced him to mature beyond his years and this was just another strange step in his journey.

Somehow, he had a vague understanding of how it must feel to be old. Life doesn't seem to get easier as time passes, rather it expands to take in more information, more obligations, and more people to love. He thought about his other self and the ache hidden behind the sparkle. It was the sadness of knowing. There were no fantasies or grand dreams in those eyes, for he had seen the best and the worst of mankind. He understood the past, fought to tame the present, and saw deeply into the future of the world. Adrian suddenly understood the message hidden in their conversation and yet, he spoke the words, "We pay a great price for the privilege…" The unspoken truth was that his life would stretch in a straight line from where he was at this moment to becoming that person three hundred years from now. The burden he was carrying seemed lighter at the thought that he would find help along the way.

He landed near the vegetable garden and noticed that the air was warm and calm, the stars glowed, and the scent of salt air was clean and fresh. The *orbs* in the old farmhouse blazed with a warm inviting glow, like candlelight flickering in the darkness, welcoming him home. Turning around and around, he realized that everything he believed in, the reasons for everything that he must do, the beginning of his path…was here.

Before he could run to the house, Brandy appeared and jumped up, his paws on Adrian's chest, licking his face, "It's so good to have you home. We all missed you and worried about you. Welcome home!"

The young *seer* hugged the red dog and they bounded up the kitchen steps, where he found the whole family seated around the oval table, laughing raucously at some joke. They all fell silent for a moment and then jumped up to hug the boy. Had he not felt so completely immersed in their love and warmth, he might have been claustrophobic. His mother wrapped her arms around him and would not let go, "We thought you were never going to come home!"

"I'm sorry to have worried you," smiled Adrian. "I honestly don't have a clue as to what day it is!"

"Well, it's a Saturday…the first Saturday in April!" replied his father. "You've been gone for almost two months!"

Adrian was dumbstruck, "Two months?"

"Yes."

"How can that be?"

His mother's smile expressed her love and relief, "It doesn't matter. All that matters is that you're home and you're safe!"

Elsie pulled away from the group and busied herself at the stove, "I might guess you're hungry. Come sit down and have a bite to eat. Tell us about everything you learned!"

The twins joined in, "Yeah, we never get to go anywhere! Tell us what happened!"

Adrian realized that he was hungry, amazingly hungry, and couldn't help wondering how two months had passed since he left with Sky and Master Chi. It seemed as if it had only been a day or two. Something strange had happened to time during his absence. Before sitting down, he made a point of hugging each member of the family one at a time, ending with his father, who had been waiting just outside the throng that enveloped him.

His father's arms were strong and Adrian felt safe and secure in his embrace, "I've missed you."

"And I missed you too," replied his son.

"Here, sit beside your mother and tell us all about your adventures!"

"Well, I wouldn't call them adventures. I guess, when I left, I'd expected to learn about fighting and survival but it wasn't like that at all. Orana told me that my greatest demons were those that I carry inside me and they'd be the hardest obstacles to overcome."

Megan piped in, "No battles with villains or creepy creatures?"

"No. Honestly, there were no real battles but the one thing I did learn was that my vulnerability and my strength both come from the same source...all of you."

There was a moment of silence around the table as each of the family absorbed the thought. "I'm not sure that I understand what you just said," said his mother.

The young *seer* smiled, "It's all about love...the love that I feel for you, for our home, for Morgan's Knot and all that it stands for. That's the reason that I've done and will do the things that are required of me. That love is also my soft spot because there's nothing that I would not do to help you or protect you...and, if you open yourself to love then you take the chance of being hurt in the process. Does that make any sense?"

John smiled, "It's the reason for everything."

"Right. One of the things that was pointed out to me was that life offers a balance of pleasure and pain, achievements and disappointments, good and bad…each can't exist without the other because we would have nothing to compare with our good fortunes or our deepest agony. Love is the motivation but, in a different light, it's also the one thing in our lives that can divert our paths from our true destiny."

Again there was quiet around the table, as everyone stared at Adrian. Elsie was the first to comment, "I think I see what you're saying, that love is the one emotion we all feel but it can pull you in opposite directions. On the one hand, it's why we're all here together…because we love each other. On the other, the love that exists between two people doesn't always end up being…healthy or beneficial for both."

George added, "I think what you're saying goes beyond that, in that the love we feel in our hearts sometimes leads us to make wrong decisions. Add to that, we're all frail and weak, when love goes badly or when love is taken away or when we find that it wasn't real to begin with."

Adrian smiled, "It's all of those things and more. I haven't had time to digest everything that was said or every lesson that was presented. I'm not sure that I'll ever get all of it but I understood enough to see my path and that was the purpose of Orana's instruction."

Brandy's nose appeared in his lap from under the table. He petted his friend's soft ears and snuck him a piece of fish from his plate.

"What's she like?" inquired Molly.

"Well, she's very old, no ancient, but, at the same time, she's like a schoolgirl in her enthusiasm and her humor. She's very wise and patient and her pink aura is incredibly strong. I could feel her before I could see her and knew that she had the ability to see inside my mind, to extract the truth, and to guide me. I knew from the first moment that there was no way I could hide anything from her. I guess the only way I can honestly describe her is to compare her to the best teacher you ever had in school times ten. While she offers knowledge and insight, she demands the most of you and will accept nothing less."

"What does she look like," asked Megan.

"She has long white hair that fans out around her like a shawl. Her blue eyes shimmer and dance as she talks, but her stare bores inside you. One moment, you feel that you're talking to an over-enthusiastic schoolgirl and, in the next instant, she could become the fiercest warrior you might ever face. I'd hate to try to stand against her, in spite of her age, because I know she'd win without much effort. She has seen...everything."

"She sounds like the perfect teacher," smiled his mother.

"She's that and more. I'd have given anything to continue but we both felt a disruption in the Balance and knew it was time for me to leave."

"Have you seen the news?" inquired George.

"I'm not sure that we were even on the same planet!" laughed Adrian.

"Well, big things are happening and you should sit down and watch the news with the girls. Oh, by the way, Dadeus, Gabrielle, Mary, and Raffe, as well as several of their engineers, arrived a couple of days ago to begin planning the first underwater modules. Soule and Amy will be here in a couple of days to begin teaching our neighbors to dive. Your mother set up a little manufacturing facility in the space behind the apothecary and everyone's being fitted for diving suits."

"Oh, that's terrific! I can't wait to see them and have a chance to dive again!"

George smiled, then turned more serious, "As I said big things are happening and you should go watch the news clip the girls saved to show you. The *seers* have gathered at the observatory. You might want to check in with Alius and the Professor."

Adrian replied solemnly, "I'll do that directly." He couldn't read George's eyes. Something was going on and it involved the *seers* but, if it was a world event being covered on the international news, then the sensation he felt while he was with Orana had been accurate.

Rushing to finish Elsie's delicious meal, he followed the girls up to their room and sat down on the floor to watch the news.

The same beautiful blond newscaster appeared before the *messenger*. "In today's headlines, infamous and self-proclaimed savior, Palloze, appeared at a gathering of Third-World leaders, proclaiming a new world order, with chilling declarations."

A video showed Zepallo, dressed in flowing white robes, standing before a bank of microphones, "Today we mark the beginning of a new order. The industrial powers have divided our world into three parts, the East, the West, and all the other nations scattered around the globe, which are impoverished and oppressed. The nations represented here include more than half of the world's population and two-thirds of the raw materials produced each year. It is our hope and our plan to join these nations together in a grand alliance to demand fair representation and equal status on the world's stage. Together, we will form a third power, a third union, that will stand for the rights of all the downtrodden peoples of the world."

Delegates from across the globe, arranged on risers behind the Dark Lord, applauded and nodded their approval.

"No longer will we permit the powers of the East and the West to steal our resources, enslave our people, or treat our governments and our institutions with disrespect and contempt! No longer will we be drawn into alliances that do not benefit our people! No longer will we bow down to the military might of the few, the rich, or the powerful!"

"Beginning tomorrow, all treaties and trade agreements between the nations of the New Coalition and the industrial powers will be subject to renegotiation. All military cooperation agreements are now null and void. All military personnel of the Suppressor Nations will be withdrawn from bases inside the borders of New Coalition countries within seventy-two hours. There will be no exceptions and National Military representatives of each nation will take control of those bases at the end of the deadline. Any military hardware of any kind, left behind, will become the property of the host nations."

"Be forewarned, the world is reacting to a thousand years of repression and, together, we will lead this transformation. The old order is finished. From this moment forward, all of the armed forces, the economic institutions, and the independent religious orders of all of these countries will speak with one voice and we will be heard!"

The newscaster reappeared, "Governments from Washington, to London, Moscow, and Peking are studying this new political force with concern. The United Nations is buzzing with activity, as these governments try to find a clear message within these announcements and, we are told, the military establishments of all of these countries have been put on high alert. We will keep you advised of any further developments."

Molly said, "Good night," and the *orb* dimmed.

"A lot has happened since you left," commented Megan. "You should probably get in touch with the Professor."

"D'ya think?"

Molly looked sad, "It's weird. Everyone on the island is so excited about the construction of the bubble world and about learning to dive, like on the Island of the Children. All of our friends are arriving and everyone seems to be filled with hope and excitement. Yet, out there in the real world, Zepallo's trying to take over the planet and we all know that whatever his plans, he'll use this opportunity to strike against the *seers*. This isn't just his forces against ours. This involves the governments and the armies of every country in the world! He could start a real war!"

Adrian put his arm around his cousin and hugged her, "I don't know enough to tell you that everything will be alright but I will tell you what I know as I learn it. In the meantime, there's no reason for the people of Morgan's Knot not to enjoy learning new things and building a new world for all of us to explore. From what we just heard, he's making threats again but that's as far as it's gone. We'll have to see what comes next."

"I think what comes next has a lot to do with the people who are running the most powerful countries on earth. Are they wise enough to stand up to Zepallo? I don't know whether I believe in them or not," said Megan.

"You do have a point," replied Adrian with a smile. "I'll go to the observatory and find out what's going on."

"I wish we could go with you," said Molly, quietly.

"I don't see why you couldn't. Let's ask Aunt...err...your mom."

The girls charged down the stairs and into the kitchen. Adrian walked into the hallway and turned to his own bedroom door, withdrawing his key from the pocket of his robes. Before he could insert it into the keyhole, the door spoke, "Ah, Master Adrian. You've been gone for quite some time. I was beginning to wonder whether you would be returning or whether they might rent out the room to someone else, in your absence."

Adrian couldn't help laughing at the sarcasm, "It's lovely to be back, I think!"

The door swung open without another word and the *orbs* by the desk and next to the bed glowed. It would feel good to take a quick shower and put on some clean clothes. The tattered blue robes had served him well but, if he had really been wearing them for two months, they were probably beyond repair. He rubbed a hand down the shredded sleeves and stopped to finger them for a moment, pondering the lesson of the demon bush, when he noticed the tears in the other sleeve suffered in his fall into the brambles.

It occurred to him that he made the transformation again from being totally focused to being relaxed and comfortable, now that he was home in his own room. He took a deep breath and closed his eyes in concentration. He saw a vision of Zepallo dressed in robes that were half black and half white, flowing behind him as he strode along a crowded street. Crowds gathered and many followed him, trying to touch him, as if he really was some sort of savior.

Adrian shook his head, wondering when he slept last. According to the timetable in the white plain, he had only gone to sleep once. How could that be?

There was no time to ponder the question. He peeled off the robes before he got through the bathroom door, turned on the water as hot as he could stand, and climbed in. The old nozzle sprayed heavy droplets from right above his head and he turned his face to the shower, allowing it to wash away the strain of his lessons.

He toweled off, grabbed some jeans, a heavy shirt, socks, and shoes and, within moments, scrambled down the stairs. His mother and father were waiting for him in the foyer.

"I know that you have to go to the observatory. I understand," said his mother calmly. "But you've just returned after two months of being away. Would it be too much to ask for a little time for us as a family?"

"I promise, once I know what's going on and what needs to be done, I'll come back and we can spend some time together," replied Adrian. "I've got to go!"

He kissed his mother and hugged his father, who smiled and shook his head. The twins burst from the kitchen, having received permission from Elsie to accompany him to the Professor's. They ran out the front door, where he stopped, put one hand on each of their shoulders, closed his eyes, and moved into the vectors.

It was only a short distance to the observatory but time enough to gauge the vectors, their sounds and the vibrations. The gentle hum rose and fell in a silky rhythm and he could not hear even the faintest grating of the dark vectors, so there would be no interceptions by anyone from the Dark Forces but, way in the background, a deep turbulence rumbled like thunder at a distance. He hugged his cousins and guided them to a soft landing at the foot of the steps to the front door of the Professor's house.

The door flew open, just as they materialized, and Alius stood, silhouetted in the glow from within, with her hands on her hips, as if she were waiting impatiently, "It's about time you showed up!"

"I only just got back," replied Adrian, sheepishly.

"You had time for dinner and a shower!" laughed the beautiful blond *seer*, as she reached out to hug her friend. "I'm so glad you're home!"

"How do you do that?"

"You do the same thing. Remember the ice cream? The problem is that you're a boy and I'm a girl. Females, obviously, feel things on a far wider field than any man ever could!" She turned to the twins, "Isn't that so?"

"Of course it's true," giggled Molly

"Boys are just the last to figure it out!" added Megan.

"I go away for a few days and come back to find that you've all become a feminists or worse, sexists!"

"I don't think it has anything to do with being chauvinistic! It's just the truth and you know it!"

"Maybe I'm not so glad I came back!" laughed Adrian, hugging Alius and stepping aside to allow Molly and Megan to enter the house. The parlor was an eclectic mix of people. Keepers from all over the world had returned to the island to work on this new problem. Adrian looked up to see one of the small people from South America standing on the top rung of the tall library ladder, trying to reach a volume on the top shelf of one of the bookcases. Before he could offer to help, Ponte turned from a bank of *messengers* that were monitoring every possible source of information, to greet the young *seer* and the twins, "I'm not surprised that you've come at precisely the right moment."

Adrian walked over and hugged the old man, who patted him on the back, just as the tiny person on the ladder took at tumble. Fortunately, two tall men, one from Africa and the other probably from northern Europe, broke his fall and set him gently on the floor. The little man in the funny hat giggled and laughed as he held up a very large book with both hands like a trophy.

Ester inserted herself between them and hugged the new arrival as if he had been gone for years. "Lovely to have you back! When there's time, you'll have to tell us all about what you've learned but, in the meantime, there's much to discover about what's happened and little to be done…yet!"

The Professor cackled like an old rooster, "Why, you're starting to sound like me!"

Adrian laughed, "One of each of you should be enough!"

"Come, come lad. We've got the *messengers* set up to monitor the international news, the military movements of the major powers, and, of course, the movements in the vectors…as well as the chatter of the Dark Forces. Unfortunately, we still haven't been able to break their cipher to get into the upper level communications but Nanchez is working on that."

"Well, at least you can tell what's going on by the quantity of messages and where they're being sent from and going to!"

"Very perceptive," laughed Nanchez, as he pushed through the crowd from the elevator behind the dining room.

Gabrielle, Dadeus, Mary and Raffe were right behind him. Adrian rushed to hug each of them and welcome them to the island, "I'm sorry I wasn't here to greet you when you arrived."

Raffe smiled, "As we understand it, you had some other things to attend to with a very important person."

"We'll talk about that when there's time. I heard that Soule and Amy are coming to teach our friends to dive. I can't wait to get back in the water."

"You've some catching up to do. I dive almost every day and I've learned so much since those first lessons. Let's go together!"

"You're on," replied Adrian. "Are the other *seers* here?"

The Professor put an arm around his shoulder, "Well, they were but they've gone off to do some research. Simian and Sammy are in

Brazil to take the temperature of the water…to see how the real citizens feel about these announcements that have been on the news. Sky has gone to Africa to meet with Shambala and Master Chi is in Beijing. They'll be back when they have new information."

"So what do we know?"

"We know that Zepallo has, somehow, organized many of the Third World Nations into a New Coalition that's making demands on the traditional powers of the East and the West. From the traffic we've been picking up from their facilities, it would seem that the Dark Forces are also talking or, perhaps, negotiating with the Industrial Powers…the other side. We have no idea what these communications are about, only that they've moved in both directions over the past twenty-four hours. We've also noticed a number of movements on the dark vectors. It would seem that he's sending emissaries to most of the Coalition Countries, as well as the major powers."

Adrian was silent for a moment, "So what you're saying is that he's playing both sides against the middle. If he plays it right, he wins no matter who loses!"

"Exactly!"

"While I was away, I learned that the elder Dark *Seers,* who controlled Zepallo, were killed in the command sub that went down during the battle on the island. He's on his own now and there are no restraints. I think it would be safe to assume that, somewhere in his plans, he'll move to eradicate the Forces of the Light, except now, he'll have conventional military might to back him up."

"He's not only invented a new game with new rules, he's increased the stakes for everyone," replied Ester.

The *orb* monitoring the news beeped and the blond newscaster's face filled the screen, "This just in, we're receiving reports from across the globe of demonstrations in support of the New Coalition and we've learned that foreign military bases are being blockaded by national army troops and civilians in many countries in the Middle East, Africa, East Asia, and South America. We go now to Thomas Connor, reporting from an American military installation in northern Saudi Arabia. Thomas, what's the latest?"

The image switched to a bearded reporter, standing in the middle of an isolated road leading to the entrance of the military facility, "I'm here at the end of this highway, at the entrance to what was assumed to be a secret American base and, as you can see, there are hundreds, if not thousands, of protesters chanting, 'America go home'. Saudi troops are barricading the road, although we're not sure whether they're protecting the facility or are, rather, a show of force to back up the New Coalition's demands for immediate withdrawal."

"So far, there have been no direct confrontations between the two sides but one must assume that the American troops, inside this fence, are on high alert."

The image changed to the demilitarized zone between North and South Korea. A Korean woman stood in front of the camera with a microphone, "Here at the DMZ, we are witnessing something that has never happened before. Citizens from the North and the South are protesting the presence of American troops and demanding their removal. On our side of the fence, American soldiers have been replaced by the South Korean army and, we are told, the Americans have been confined to their barracks until they receive further instructions from Washington."

Again, the video cut to the Prime Minister's residence at 10 Downing Street. "Black limousines have formed a queue, as dignitaries and officials arrived for meetings to determine the validity of the demands, made by Palloze and the New Coalition, and to draft a response."

A similar scene followed, with long black cars coming in and out of the gates at the White House in Washington. "The report is much the same, here in Washington, where President Bartlett and his advisors have been meeting all day with military officials and ambassadors from many of the New Coalition countries. Although there has been no official announcement, one un-named source told us that, so far, every representative from the Coalition countries who has arrived, demanded the immediate withdrawal of American and Allied forces from their territories, produced documents to formally end all trade and treaty agreements, and then departed, without waiting for a formal reply."

The blond newscaster reappeared, "We have nothing with which to compare these events in the entire history of the world and, we might assume, that we are seeing the beginning of something that will change the course of our future."

"In related news, the stock markets across the globe suffered significant losses today, as frightened investors moved their accounts into cash and precious metals. Wall street closed just after 11:30 this morning, after the index fell more than one thousand points in the first hour of trading."

There was a pause, as she listened to new information on her headset, "We have just learned that all shipments of oil have been suspended by the OPEC nations until further notice. Is this the first step in a new economic balance in the world or just a short-term move to bolster the demands of the New Coalition and raise prices? We don't have the answer to that question, yet, but we must assume that the term 'business as usual' is a thing of the past. We will return, shortly, with more."

"It's a good thing that we don't depend on oil for our power!" said Megan.

"Good point," replied the Professor, his complexion decidedly ashen, "but this is going to change the balance of power in the world and I'm not sure that, in the end, it will be for the betterment of anyone, other than Zepallo."

"I think it offers a better chance of chaos!" thundered Nanchez, with his usual talent for understatement.

Adrian sat down at the dining room table and tried to focus on the tone of the vibrations being emitted across the world by all of the humans combined. That distant resonance was thrashing to the surface, faint whispers merging into a crescendo. There had been no reason to believe that the lessons learned on his journey would be put to use quite so soon.

Alius sat down opposite him, "I know that look. What are you thinking?"

"I wish we had time for me to explain some of what I've been through in the past few days…or…couple of months. I still haven't figured out how time got so skewed. Anyway, what I was thinking was that the last lesson concerned the End of Times. An old book dropped out of the sky and when I opened it, I found it was completely empty, except for the last page, which said, simply, 'The End.' The title on the cover read 'The End of Times' and the author…'Everyman'."

Alius looked across the table with curiosity, "What did it mean?"

"I talked with Orana about it, for a long time, and she said that the future was up to all of us, not just you and me, but everyone on the planet. We're the authors and our actions…or lack of action, will determine what fills those pages."

"Little did you know what was happening while you were gone!"

Adrian smiled, "Touché! I wish I could have been here with you but I hope we might all benefit from the things I learned. The current situation seems to be my first test."

Ponte, Ester, Dadeus, Raffe, Mary, and Gabrielle sat down with the two *seers*, as the rest of the Keepers crammed into the dining room. Tic jumped up on the table and walked over to nuzzle against Adrian, who picked him up and held the old cat against his chest.

"It's nice to have you home," purred Tic.

"It's nice to be home with friends like you!"

"We don't really know what's happening or, for that matter, how we might affect the chain of events that are unfolding in most of the capitals of the world. You children have already demonstrated Zepallo's true character, when you were in the United Nations, but that doesn't seem to have made much difference in the reception he's received from the Third World countries, who have aligned themselves with him," said Gabrielle with slow deliberation.

"You'd hope they'd have seen the truth," moaned Alius.

Dadeus interrupted, "I don't think that it's a matter of seeing his true character, rather, an alliance of convenience. He needs a global front for his secret plans to dominate the world. All of these countries need a belligerent spokesman for their cause. It surprises me that the third world nations have not allied themselves before. The industrial powers have abused and denigrated them for centuries."

"They had to have a rallying point, someone to bring them all together to stand up to the major powers and they're in an enviable position. The United States, the European Union, The Russian bloc, and the Chinese could join together and attack individual countries, as examples, but the downside is that such an action would drive the rest of the countries of the New Coalition together, in an even stronger bond. I don't envy the Prime Minister of England, the President of the United States, or the Chairman of the People's Republic of China. No matter what they decide to do, they lose."

"You're right," said Ponte, "and all of this just magnifies one of the problems in our world. Governments speak for their people but they are not truly the people's voice."

Adrian had been quiet, listening to the adults, "I think I see what you're saying, whether the populations of all of the countries of the world agree with their governments or not, they're forced to support them, because they really have no direct voice in the events or the...direction their governments take. It's always been assumed that the people needed representation. Without it, there would be anarchy...but maybe anarchy isn't as bad as evil leaders."

Ponte stared at the young *seer*, "That was very deep for someone of your age! What did you learn on your journey?"

"Mostly I learned about the demons that live inside me," replied Adrian with a bashful grin.

One of the Keepers from India spoke up, "In my country, which, incidentally, is allied with the New Coalition, a great majority of our people live at or below the poverty level. To them, this is long overdue, although I am absolutely sure they have no way of seeing the broader implications of this movement. In their eyes, this is vindication of the anger and frustration that they feel in their lack of opportunity to escape a very meager existence."

An American Indian, in full headdress of eagle feathers, agreed, "All people feel these things, even in the United States. Our people are treated, at best, as inferior second-class citizens. I'm sure that they're sympathetic to this New Coalition and hope that, somehow, the events that are unfolding will benefit them in the long run."

A tall, very dark man from Central Africa added, "Our allegiances are, first, to our tribes and, second, to our nations. It might be worth noting that most of the third world countries were created when the colonial powers drew lines on a map, without regard to the ethnic loyalties of the people who lived in those places. The mother, whose child is starving because the wars in our countries have ravaged the farmlands, poisoned the waters, and killed off entire generations over the past several centuries, has no interest in global power. She just wants to find a way to feed her child. None of the powerful countries in the world could be bothered to defend us or help in the recoveries, when the wars were finished. To the common person, The President of the United States, or the Prime Minister of Great Britain, or the leader in the Kremlin are enemies, because of their complete disregard for human needs, let alone human rights. Whatever aid was offered, came at a price, one-sided programs to steal our natural resources or cheap labor in exchange for a dam or a road or inadequate shipments of food or medical assistance. I'm sure this holds true for many of the countries that have joined in this new union. To them, this is self-defense."

Adrian flashed back to his conversation with himself. "It's all about fear."

"I'll agree with that," replied the African Keeper.

"Explain what you mean," instructed Ester.

"I'll skip the explanation of how I came to that conclusion but basically what it means is that most people live in fear...fear of not having enough or not being enough or having someone come and take whatever they do have. I think it applies to everyone, rich or poor, educated or illiterate. Everyone in the normal world has to contend with the struggle to maintain and defend what they have."

"I see your point," inserted Ponte.

"They fear each other, their governments, terrorists, the power of other nations, even their religious institutions. The leaders of nations and religions have used fear to control and manipulate the masses for centuries, yet there have been very few times when the common people have joined together to be heard as one voice. Taking it a step further, that mentality allows those leaders to use the 'us verses them' message to galvanize their groups and to justify their actions."

"Hitler blamed the Communists and the Jews for all the problems that Germany suffered after World War One, when, in reality, neither group had much of a hand in the tragedies their country went through during those years. His message came down to good Germans against those evil people who are repressing us and it worked," said Ester.

"Exactly," replied Adrian. "This current situation will escalate until there's a major military confrontation or...the world hears the voice of the people...all of the people."

"The leaders of all the nations are hamstrung by the positions they hold and the alliances they have formed across the globe. This is not only about political power but, perhaps more critical, about economic control. There is only one person who can stand up in front of the world and denounce Zepallo for what he is, Ponte looked up at his favorite student solemnly, "are you sure you're ready for that?"

Adrian was quiet for a minute, gazing down at the floor planks. He could feel everyone staring at him, waiting for his reply. "Why is it that it always comes down to doing what must be done?"

"Because that's the person that you are," said Alius quietly.

Tic purred, "All you have to do is to convince the entire world of the beauty of the Balance."

"That's easy for you to say!"

Chapter 6

Adrian and Alius walked out into the night and sat down on the grass. High in the sky, a silver moon illuminated the island with a soft, cool glow. A million stars twinkled and a gentle breeze carried a salty scent from the ocean. It was good to be home.

"Was it all that you might have hoped it would be?" inquired Alius.

"I don't really know how to answer that question because, as Orana said, the lessons for each individual are different, depending on their character and purpose. If you had a chance to go, your instruction would be completely different than mine."

The beautiful *seer* leaned back on her elbows and stared up at the sky, "Were you frightened?"

"A few times but I think the more important lessons made me look inside myself."

"So, there wasn't any fighting or yucky villains?"

"No, the only confrontation that I had was with Zepallo and my mother."

"That combination doesn't compute!"

"I agree but, at the time, it seemed very real."

"What happened?"

"I fell asleep and dreamed that my mother had fallen in love with Zepallo and they wanted me to join them to conquer the world."

"Did you fight?"

"I couldn't without hurting my mother. Instead, it became a stand off… Zepallo held his crystal sword so it barely touched the end of my nose and I held my blaster, ready to fire. Stalemate."

Alius leaned over and inspected Adrian's nose. "Have you noticed that you have a little scuff, right on the tip of your nose?"

"No!" replied Adrian, as he reached up to touch his nose and felt a small scab.

"Maybe it wasn't a dream."

"It was a dream because I woke up and Phaschin was sitting on my chest, pecking at my nose!"

"Who is Fashion?"

"It isn't fashion, like fancy dresses and all that, it's P-h-a-s-c-h-i-n. He's a beautiful parrot, who guided me through a forest. Other than a very odd sense of humor, he was a good companion and guide."

"Maybe he scratched your nose."

"Could be," replied Adrian reached up to touch this tip of his nose again. "That was when I realized that my strength and my weaknesses come from my love for all of you and for the Power of the Light."

Alius was quiet for a moment, "What was the weirdest thing that you encountered?"

Adrian paused for a moment and smiled, "Probably...talking to myself as a three-hundred year old man. The funny part was that we were both naked!"

"You're kidding!"

"No, we had a long conversation sitting cross-legged on an endless white plain and, although he didn't tell me everything I could look forward to, he did give me some insights. He told me that the women in my life were the ones who hold the keys to my happiness and success."

"Well, that seems kind of obvious!"

"You're certainly in an uppity mood tonight," laughed Adrian.

"I guess I'm just glad to have you back. Even though we knew that you'd be well cared for, we all worried. We couldn't help it."

The two *seers* were quiet, staring up at the stars. That shiver raced up Adrian's spine again, ending with a sharp sting at the base of his skull that blurred his vision. He closed his eyes to regain his balance and saw the vision of Zepallo, dressed in black and white robes, rushing down a street, followed by a crowd of people.

"What is it?" asked Alius.

"I see Zepallo running down a street, surrounded by people, and he's wearing robes that are half-black and half-white. I don't know what it means."

"Perhaps you're seeing beyond the façade that he's presenting to the world. We know the demon who hides behind the white robes and that charming exterior."

"Maybe...but I almost feel that I'm supposed to do something with what I'm sensing. I just don't know what."

"You will, it will come to you."

"I don't know that there's much more we can do here. It's getting late and I should probably make sure the twins get back to the House of the Four Seasons before the grownups get in a twit."

"Let's meet tomorrow morning," suggested Alius, with a smile, as she leaned over and kissed his cheek. "I sure have missed you."

"And I've missed you. I wish we could have gone together but I hope you'll have a chance to learn from her. She's very wise."

"Let's deal with first things first."

"Right," replied Adrian, as he stood and reached to help Alius to her feet. That moment brought a flashback to the first time they had talked, after their battle on the mountain. He was still amazed at her beauty and that cold determination hiding behind her pale eyes and held her close for a long moment.

They walked back into the crowded parlor, hand-in-hand, and found the twins in a deep discussion with a very old Chinese woman and one of the tiny people from South America.

Adrian whispered to Megan, "I think we ought to be heading back. I told my parents that I'd spend some time with them this evening and it's already late."

"Right then, let's be off," giggled his cousin.

Adrian found Ponte standing in front of the bank of *orbs*, talking with Nanchez in low tones. "We've got to head back to the House of the Four Seasons but I'll be back in the morning, if that's alright with you?"

The two Keepers patted him on the back, "You've probably been through a lot in the past two months. There doesn't seem to be anything that anyone can do until we see what happens next. Come by when you get up. We'll all be here."

Adrian hugged his friends and led the twins outside. They levitated back to the House of the Four Seasons but found that everyone had already gone to bed.

They grabbed *orbs* from the carrier at the bottom of the stairs and tiptoed to their rooms. Molly giggled quietly, "Thank you for taking us. It was much more interesting than waiting for you to report back on what was happening!"

"There doesn't seem to be much that anyone can do at the moment but I don't think this calm will last for long. I'll see you in the morning."

"Good night," whispered the girls in unison.

Adrian stepped to his door, which opened silently, peeled off his clothes, and found his nightshirt hanging on a peg on the back of the bathroom door.

Slipping between clean sheets felt wonderful. *"How is possible that I've been gone for two months?"* He wondered, *"and how is possible that I've only slept for a few hours in all that time?"*

He looked around the room and thought about all the curious and terrifying things that happened since the first lonely night he spent in this house. His life had taken a new direction, one that no one could have predicted, yet it seemed that his path had always been there before him. He just had no way of understanding it until fate forced him to take those first steps.

Bits and pieces of his conversation with his older self crept through his mind. How could he possibly live to be three hundred years old? It seemed impossible until he thought about Orana and all that she had seen in her long lifetime.

He heard her final words, "There are two things that you should take into consideration. First, that no one...and I honestly mean no one, understands the responsibility for which you and I have volunteered. I understand because I have lived these many years and I have led the good fight through the centuries. You will understand because your path is predestined...you will take on your enemies because, as you say, there is no other choice."

The words echoed through the darkness, as he allowed himself to descend into that mystifying state between sleep and consciousness. Again, he felt that electric shock run up his spine to detonate the sharp pain at the point where his neck supported his skull. The vision of Zepallo was repeated, like a clip from a movie running over and over. *"There's something there that I'm supposed to understand, some message that's eluding me...something that I must do...*"

He fell into a deep but fitful sleep and dreamed in flashes of the lessons in the white plain. Nothing was complete, the snippets did not fit together...and yet, somehow, they did. There was a common thread running through each of the chapters of his training but his dreams would not allow him to see beyond his experiences to tie them all together.

Dawn broke, cold and gray. There was no sunshine streaming through limp curtains hanging at the window, so Adrian pulled the covers up over his head and tried to go back to sleep. It was no use, his mind was already racing, viewing the news clip that he watched with the girls, editing the few comments that he heard while he was at the observatory, searching for something useful.

"On the one hand, what's happening will probably empower and reward the people of all of those Third-World countries who have no other options. On the other, anything that involves Zepallo can only lead to darkness and destruction." Adrian paused, pondering, *"I wonder whether there is a third path...one that allows the world to become more equal, more fair...? That's a creative possibility!"*

He jumped out of bed and walked over to the window and pulled back the curtains to expose the gray misty morning. A gentle fog rolled across the fields, softening the sharp lines and muting the shadows.

He pulled off his nightshirt, climbed into his clothes, and scrambled down the stairs to the kitchen, where he found everyone gathered around the table.

"Ah, it's nice to see your face!" laughed Aunt Elsie, as she got up to fetch a plate for her nephew.

Adrian walked over to the stove and gave her a hug before he sat down. "How's everyone this morning?"

His mother leaned over to accept a kiss, "We're all fine. There's much too much to do!"

"You haven't told me about your new workshop!"

"Well, it's a bit cramped but there's enough room for the scanner and I've found lots of help from the ladies from the seamstress shop. I'm afraid we've taken over part of the funhouse for a storehouse for the materials but we'll clear that out as soon as we're finished sewing the suits."

Adrian turned to his father and his uncle, "How's the planning going for the domes?"

The two men laughed, "It'll take a bit of organization but I think we're on the right track. Gabrielle and Dadeus have been guiding us through the planning stages. We've built a road from the foundry to the beach and Travis has fitted one of the trawlers to drive the first pilings."

His father added, "If all goes well, we should have the first dome enclosed by fall."

"That's great," replied Adrian, between bites of egg and toast. "I can't wait to dive with Raffe. It's been ages!"

"Oh, you'll get your chance. There's something for everyone to do on the site!"

"More work!"

"Did you really expect anything less?" inquired Elsie with a grin.

Molly piped up, "You'll probably have to go on one of your missions, while the rest of us do all the hard stuff!"

"I don't honestly know what I'll have to do about the current situation but I'm more than willing to help!"

The children cleared the table and washed the dishes, while the adults wandered off to attend to their own chores.

Adrian found his mother sitting on the bottom step outside the kitchen rinsing fresh lettuce and greens from the garden. He sat down beside her. "I'm sorry that I didn't get back before you went to bed last night."

"I understand," smiled Sara. "You have your own responsibilities, although the current situation frightens me. So far, your missions have pitted you against Zepallo and the Dark Forces. Now the world is on the brink of a war like no other and I'm not sure that one lone boy can stop the momentum that's underway."

"I honestly don't know what I can do but I'm beginning to find an insight to the path that I have to follow. It all depends on what the world powers decide to do. Will they give in to the demands of the Coalition or will they dig in their heels and resist? If they do resist, will it be military, economic, or purely political? There's no way of knowing."

"You know that I can't help but see you as my young son. Do you realize it's been just a year since we started our journey to Vancouver?"

"That was something else that came up while I was in the planes. I guess the first time I realized the change that I was going through was on the way back from the Island of the Children. We were almost home and I was standing on the bow of the Sparrow, wondering whether I could ever just be a normal kid again. Morgan came up and put her arm around me and reminded me that I couldn't go back to being the person I was when I arrived on this island. I had to choose between being one of the kids or being myself and, when I thought about it, there really wasn't much choice. I'd already taken the first steps on the path to becoming a *seer* and I really couldn't go back."

His Mother was quiet for a moment, "Tell me about your trip."

Adrian smiled, "It wasn't what I expected." He paused, trying to find the words that might explain what he had been through. "I don't really know how to describe it. I guess I assumed that I'd be drilled in weapons or powers or tactics and it was none of those. Each lesson was about my fears and weaknesses."

"What was the most powerful thing you learned?"

Sara's son watched the gray mist rolling across the fields to the south. He wasn't sure whether he should discuss the dream or avoid the subject. "Each part was completely different from the others. There was one, where I learned that defending the Balance and the Powers was not enough. Rather, I understood that this planet is a living organism that supports every living creature, every living thing. I have to make the people of the world understand that we have to start taking care of our world or all life will cease to exist. The Powers, whether Dark or Light, won't make any difference if we destroy our home.

The most amusing, and perhaps the most enlightening, was a conversation I had with myself as a three hundred year old man. The other me didn't give me all the answers but he did tell me that, in the end, we'll look back and be proud of our accomplishments. He pointed out that the things that I do in my lifetime will affect the course of history and the lives of many. One point he made was that the women in my life will determine my happiness and success and that I already know the person that I'll marry…but he wouldn't tell me who!"

"I should hope not," laughed his mother, "there are some things that you have to find for yourself!"

"I agree, although at the time, I struggled to figure it out."

"What was the darkest lesson?"

"I'm not really sure how to describe it," began Adrian. "I fell asleep, actually, it was the only time that I slept during my time with Orana. Anyway, I dreamed that you had fallen in love with Zepallo and the two of you were trying to convince me to join you in conquering the world."

Sara gasped, "You know that can't be real!"

"It seemed very real and it ended up as a stalemate. Zepallo held his crystal sword to the tip of my nose and I held my blaster, ready to fire...but I couldn't because you were in the way. It was a stalemate."

Adrian's mother leaned forward to inspect the tip of his nose. "You've got a little scab, right there on your nose!"

"I don't really understand that either," replied her son, blushing. "The other thing that I can't quite figure out is how I could possibly have been gone for two months. It seemed like a few days at most."

Sara looked out at the fields, "Perhaps time works differently in the planes. When you left, we were in the depths of winter, now the fields are full of spring growth. Time passed too slowly and, to tell you the truth, I missed you terribly."

Mother and son wrapped their arms around each other in a long, gentle hug. Adrian could feel her heart beating and he could smell the faintest hint of her perfume. He closed his eyes and felt like the boy who had cried when his parents left him on this island. It seemed a very long time ago.

Chapter 7

Zepallo materialized at the mouth of the frigid entrance, his white robes shedding their luster through shades of gray until they returned to black. The charming smile and the gentle but determined gaze transformed, the slender lips curled into a sneer to match the chill of his icy stare.

The Dark Lord scanned the sky. The moon had yet to rise over the mountains and the stars looked brighter than usual. *"Our time has come,"* he thought, turning into the tunnel and ignoring the salute of the two sentries guarding the entry.

This newest facility far surpassed any of their former lairs. The technicians were building connections that had never been possible with the old systems. The latest generation could be programmed to tap in or out of the vectors at any point on the planet, focusing power locally or bridging them together for special projects.

Shafts of blue and purple light rippled along the corridor, creating the illusion that the channel was breathing, as if it had a life of its own. In a way, it did. Although the technicians were constantly updating the programs, the system ran independently. It was more than just a computer, reaching out along the vectors to touch every point of interest, it burrowed into the most secure systems of the most powerful nations and intercepted signals from every satellite in the heavens…and he was its master.

Senior Regents, Cadeau and Regis, met him at the elevator that would descend to the command center more than a thousand feet beneath the level of the entrance. There would be no invasion here.

"The news reports of your journey are very positive. They fawned over your message of honor and dignity, freeing the suppressed masses, and challenging the authority and power of the ruling nations," gushed Regis.

"Add to that, facing down the most powerful military establishments without firing a shot!" injected Cadeau, with a chuckle.

"Gentlemen, this is only the first step in a long and complicated strategy. Certainly, we've made a good first performance but there are many ways we might be foiled along the way, not the least of which are the Forces of the Light and young Adrian!"

"Our system touches the Black Crystal on Morgan's Knot, which they are using not only for power but also to monitor the dark planes and the vectors. We know at least half of what they're interested in and where they're looking. For instance, we know that they're monitoring our communications but we have every reason to believe that they haven't broken into the secure networks."

"So, you're saying that they can see traffic but they can't understand the messages that are being sent?" inquired Zepallo.

"That's right," said Regis.

"Then they can track the volume of messages being sent in and out of our facilities around the world, which gives them a clue to the concentration of our forces and our command centers. That's interesting, it could prove useful at some future time."

"How do you mean, Sire?" asked Cadeau.

"I mean that we could load up specific circuits with false messages to misdirect their attention. That should be obvious to you! After all, you are my Senior Security Technician, are you not?"

"Yes, proudly!"

"Then do your job!" shouted Zepallo, levitating to the podium suspended in mid-air at the center of the dome. Thousands of spherical workstations floated around the control center in concentric circles from the highest point in the dome to the floor, each moving through the space independently of the others. If several technicians were working on a project together, they could link their bubbles near a giant screen that displayed, in three dimensions, the sum of their efforts.

Here and there, luminescent spheres nestled together, like a small swarm of purple bees tussling to enter their hive at the same time.

As each new piece was added to the project, bright flashes confirmed the connections, reminiscent of sparks flying from welder's arcs during the industrial revolution more than a century ago. When the entire task was completed, the huge screen would display a beautiful black diamond shimmering in a pool of purple luminance. The team's success was duly noted in their records. Survival was not the only perk to be enjoyed by those who contributed and obeyed.

The Dark Lord was still awestruck by the beauty and functionality of this grand space. Master *Seers*, Wonac and Ptolemy, had been lost in the command submarine during the battle on Morgan's Knot and there had been little resistance, when Zepallo took the reins of the Council with a firm hand and a wink to his assurances that he would avoid unnecessary confrontations. Secretly, he admired their wisdom and restraint...to a point...but they demanded that the Powers be used as tradition dictated and impeded his efforts to move their technology and their goals out of the past and into the future. Neither would have dreamed of an alliance that represented more than half of the population of the planet! No councilor, in the entire history of Legio Obscurum, would have dared to solicit or accept the support of the masses in the real world.

He paused for a moment, reflecting on those who believed in the Power of the Light. He knew that, sooner or later, they would have to attempt to rise against him. Their power was fractured and insignificant compared to the will of the masses, access to clandestine nuclear programs in a dozen countries, and a unified army that would number in the millions. *"Young Adrian is wise for his young age and, potentially, could be the strongest seer in generations but this battle will not be won by one seer over another. This is a war for control of the world! He can not win and I will not lose, but it wouldn't hurt to have a little insurance!"*

Chapter 8

President Bartlett picked up the receiver of the secure line that was maintained between the White House and 10 Downing Street, in London.

The Prime Minister's crisp accent masked his concern. "I'd say good morning but my guess is that neither of us got much sleep last night and, for our part, it's rather gloomy outside today."

"It's about the same here," replied the president with a small smile. He had always admired Prime Minister Langdon's ability to find humor in the darkest moments.

"What are you hearing on your end?"

"Well, the market went through the floor yesterday and we've got riots at most of our installations in South Korea, the Philippines, Afghanistan, Iraq, Saudi Arabia, and Guantánamo. You name it, they have crowds screaming for our complete and immediate withdrawal."

"How are the oil reserves going to hold up?"

"My people tell me that we can continue normal activities for sixty to ninety days before we have to tap our reserves. After that, who knows?"

"We have the advantage of our wells in the North Sea and the fact that United Kingdom is, for the most part, self-sufficient but our experts suggest that we'll begin feeling the pinch not long after you do."

"There has to be a sane solution to this problem!" exclaimed Bartlett.

"I think the solution might have started two or three-hundred years ago, when our ancestors decided to start slicing up vast sections of the world and distributing them to their patrons!"

"You do have a point, although the Kings and Queens of England certainly took more than their fair share!"

"Ah, but the Colonies have made up for lost time! Damned Yanks!"

The president could not restrain himself and burst out laughing. "Our ancestors did as much damage as any!"

"We can't do anything about the past, my friend, but I'm afraid that we will be held accountable for what happens now and in the future. Neither of us wants to go down in the history books as the shepherds who led our flocks to slaughter!"

"What do we know about this Palloze person? Where did he come from and how did he galvanize so many countries without anyone noticing?"

"Our people have been looking into that and they've come up with some very sketchy details. The first reference was more than thirty years ago, when it is believed he was a priest at the Vatican. At the time, there were rumors that he was being groomed to eventually move closer to the Papal throne but, as the story goes, one day he just disappeared and no one heard anything further about him, until he showed up at the United Nations, talking disarmament and equality for the peoples of all nations."

"Wasn't that the speech that was interrupted by that young boy and the animals?"

"One and the same. The United Nations will never recover. Now we have to debate with wild creatures. Actually, it might be preferable to dealing with wild people," laughed the Prime Minister.

"What happened to that boy?"

"No one knows. He disappeared and hasn't been heard from since. Perhaps, if we could find him, he could give us some insight into this villain and his true intentions!"

"I'll agree with that. Let's put our best people on finding him, wherever he might be. He could be the key to the solution to this mess!"

"Roger that, I'll see what I can find out on this end."

"Let's keep this line open, we'll need to talk later in the day and pray that we can make some progress with at least a few of our old allies."

"Don't count on it. It's too soon for any of them to start caving in. They want to see how the hand plays out before committing completely to one side or the other. At this point, the Coalition must look like a safe bet. There's strength in numbers and they do have the numbers!"

"More than half of the world's population. It's almost dividing the world into two hemispheres on either side of the Tropic of Cancer…the North and the South. The global version of the American Civil War on a grand scale!"

"Let's hope that it doesn't come to that!"

"I'll call you later," said the president solemnly, as he hung up the phone. He turned in his chair to gaze out the window. Yellow street lamps warmed the dull glow of morning hanging low over the rolling fog, little bursts of hope in a bitter gray smear across the city. Bustling traffic was reduced to a trickle of quivering headlamps, damp sidewalks untrampled by wandering crowds of the patriotic and the curious…as if the entire population of the city was holding its breath, waiting to see what might happen in the next instant or the next minute.

Over the course of twenty-four hours, the center of power in the world had shifted and, for the moment, maintaining the most powerful armed forces on the planet had very little value. As a former economics professor at Harvard, he knew too well that all world conflicts came down to the same few causes. The first, the primary reason, was always economics. Money could buy power, influence decisions, overthrow governments, and move reluctant populations through the power of the media or sermons delivered from the pulpit.

This was no different. The Coalition countries held more than seventy-five percent of the world's natural resources, a vast majority of the oil reserves that fueled production in the industrialized nations, and more than half the humans…and most of them could care less about the United States or any of the other powerful countries that ruled the world for the past several centuries. To them, this whole movement was sweet retribution for the arrogance and cruelty displayed by wealthy nations.

Although they could not understand or appreciate the effect it would have on everyone in every country, their point was well taken.

He punched the intercom to his secretary, "Natalie, would you get me the Director of the CIA and see if someone on the staff can come up with a tape of that young boy who interrupted Palloze's speech at the United Nations several months ago."

Moments later, the intercom buzzed, "I have Director Sloan on the line."

"Thank you, I'll take the call," replied the president. "Don, how are things on your end?"

"As confusing as ever. We're tapping every source that we've ever had in every country in the world. Those in the Coalition countries are hesitant to talk with us at the moment. I don't doubt that they fear for their lives, especially under these…unusual circumstances. My people are trying their damnedest but this is uncharted territory."

"I understand. It's certainly a new balance," said President Bartlett. "Don, I have a favor to ask and I think we should keep this quiet, if that's alright with you."

"Certainly, Mr. President."

"Do you remember that boy who interrupted the speech that Palloze was giving at the United Nations?"

"I certainly do. That was one of the lighter moments in the recent history of diplomacy."

"I agree. My question is whether we know who that young man was and where we might find him?"

"To tell you the truth, I have no idea but I'll see what I can find out."

"As I said, I want to keep this quiet. Whether he knew it or not, he did the world an enormous favor and I don't want to be responsible for putting him in danger. I just think he might have some…insight that could guide us through this current dilemma."

"I understand your concern and I'll approach this inquiry with a delicate hand. I'll get back to you as soon as possible."

"Thank you, Mr. Director," said the president, as he hung up the phone.

Natalie buzzed his intercom. "Mr. President, Miss Granger is here to see you with the videotape that you requested."

"Send her right in!"

The president was out of his chair and halfway to the door, when his Press Secretary knocked and walked into the room waving the videotape in her hand. "You wanted to see this tape, Mr. President?"

"Yes, I did. Would you put it on the television for me?"

"Certainly, Mr. President."

Ms. Granger fast-forwarded the tape through the introduction and stopped as Zepallo began his speech.

"I come as an ambassador for peace," he began, in a deep sonorous voice, soliciting sympathy and support with polished eloquence. "I bring a vision of the future that does not include arms or war. I see a world where the rich reach down to assist the poor, where famine and terrorism will become unpleasant memories, as we move into the future together."

The audience erupted with a thunderous applause.

"We are one world. We are one people. Colonialists drew the borders that separate us, generations ago, for their own political and economic gain. It's time for a new vision...a new path for all the people of the world.

Again, the room exploded with applause.

Zepallo raised a sheaf of papers above his head. "I have proposals from North Korea, Palestine, the Taliban in Afghanistan, the rebels of Columbia, and many others. They're willing to meet with their foes to bring a final and lasting peace to their regions. My question is...are the leaders of the most powerful nations in the world willing to work with these patriots to put an end to war and to build a future for all mankind? Or are we going to continue down this path that will surely lead to more misery and destruction?"

The applause was deafening.

"Over the past one-hundred years, vast resources have been dedicated to manufacturing weapons and the sole purpose for those arms is to enable us to kill each other more efficiently. The industrialized nations have amassed enough guns and bombs to annihilate the entire population of the world several times over. I suggest that, if those funds were diverted to help the destitute of the world, there would be no reason for war!

The news reporters have referred to me as a messiah. If they want to refer to me as a messenger of peace, I will not object. I've been asked which religion I represent. It is my belief that, no matter which corner of the world you come from, which religion you follow, or the traditions of your ancestors, we all worship the same God. Does anyone really believe that you must be a Christian…or a Jew…or a Muslim…to be admitted to heaven? I believe in one God and one world and I ask you to join with me to bring peace and prosperity to every soul who inhabits this planet!"

The president was growing impatient, "Skip this part. We know that the man is a zealot. I'm more interested in the young man who interrupted this nonsense!"

The tape zipped forward and stopped, just as the animals began moving down the isles. A young woman stood with the group of homeless people before the podium, asking questions of Palloze.

Suddenly, the camera panned to follow a young girl flying through the air and hovering with the young man in the blue robes just behind the speaker.

The boy yelled, "This man represents everything evil in our world. Do not believe him! Do not follow him!"

"We come from a place where the humans and the animals work together in a perfect balance. These animals will not harm you. They're here to demonstrate the best of our world and the future of your world. This man, Palloze, as he calls himself, wants only to rule, to dominate, and to destroy. He is no messiah, he's the devil in human form!" shouted the girl.

Palloze turned, raised his hand, and pointed something at the boy, who ducked to his right, as a pulsing blast rushed through the air and struck a large bronze plaque on the far wall. The crest exploded and clattered to the floor.

The girl screamed, "You see, this messiah attacks children!"

There was some commotion behind Palloze, whose hand swung toward another young man in a white suit and a black man who seemed to be attending to him. A flash passed over their heads and exploded on the wall behind them.

The animals pressed forward but the birds and insects were first to reach the man at the podium. A close-up showed them buzzing and screeching around his head. Palloze thrashed his arms, to ward off the attack, and stumbled off the podium. The camera zoomed in, as he scanned the chaos roiling through the assembly room, bowed his head, and vanished.

The boy and the girl, hovering defensively in mid-air, floated around the stage and turned to say something to the young man in white and the black man, who was protecting him. Then the boy whistled, the animals turned their full attention, and everything in the room seemed to stop moving.

The youngster in the blue robes reached up and pulled the microphone down to his level, "Ladies and gentlemen, that concludes our entertainment for the evening!"

The camera panned back to show the delegates and members of the gallery and, slowly, applause spread through the room, as calm was restored.

"As I said earlier, these animals represent the natural world. I promise, they will not harm you. Please feel free to pet them, talk with them, and accept them as your friends. There's much that you might learn from them."

The video panned across the room to show the animals and the delegates conversing. In the background, the boy in the blue robes, accompanied by the girl, the boy in the white suit, the black man, and the homeless people disappeared through an entrance at the back of the Assembly Room.

Ms. Granger stopped the video.

"I think we should have paid much closer attention to this man and the boy. Everyone was so astonished by this whole episode they seem to have ignored the fact that people, other than Superman and Peter Pan, don't fly. We have to find that boy, he might be the key to unlocking the puzzle."

"I'll see what I can do."

"I've got Don Sloan working on it and I hope that he's being very quiet in his inquiries. This boy might be able to help but not if we expose him to the whole world!"

"I see your point Mr. President. I'll make some calls to see what I can find out and I'll be very careful in my approach."

"Thank you. He won't be of any use to us or anyone else if he's dead!"

~

Several hours later, Natalie buzzed the president. "I have the Canadian Ambassador to the United Nations, Anthony Robbins, on the phone. He won't tell me what it concerns. Should I tell him that you'll call him back?"

"No, I'll take the call. Thank you, Natalie."

The president picked up the receiver, "Tony! How are you?"

"I think that all of us might be better, Mr. President."

"How can I help you?"

"Well, I've received a very quiet inquiry into the young man who was responsible for that show in the General Assembly, several months ago."

"Yes."

"I can't tell you who he is, because I don't know, but I think I know of a way that we might be able to reach him."

"I'm listening."

"There was a group of homeless people who spoke, just before that circus parade marched into the chambers. I offered some assistance to them and am pleased to say that the young woman and her child now have legal status in my country and are being well cared for. I honestly don't know why but her friends refused my offer of assistance. Something about having to protect a treasure."

"I wish our people had stepped in!"

"I think it's possible that she might be able to contact them. She told me that the young woman had given her an email address, where she could be reached."

"Mr. Ambassador, I think the future of the world might depend on my having a conversation with that young man. Could you see what you can do?"

"Yes, Mr. President."

"And Tony…do it very quietly."

"As you wish," replied the Canadian Ambassador.

Chapter 9

Sara reluctantly released her son from a hug, "I take it that you're off to the observatory?"

"Yes, although I'm not sure what I can do to help at this point."

"You just do what you feel is right, the rest will come."

"What are you doing today?"

"Well, I have to hurry to finish rinsing these greens, then I'm off to the workshop to make sure that everything is on schedule. We'll be needing as many divers as possible and they can't begin their training until the suits are ready." Leaning back, she sized up her son, "It wouldn't surprise me to find that you've outgrown your suit. Come by later and we'll run you through the scanner."

"I can't wait to dive with Raffe. It's been so long!"

"I know what you mean."

"Oh, by the way. I tore up the sleeves of my blue robes. When you have a minute, could you see whether they can be mended?"

"Certainly. I'll tend to it tonight," relied his mother with a smile. Considering Adrian's independence, it was a pleasure to be needed. "Will you be home for dinner?"

"I'll make a point of it!" said Adrian, as he stood, leaned down to kiss his mother, and walked out onto the lawn. A moment later, he vanished.

~

The observatory was quiet, as he entered the front door. It seemed that most of the Keepers had left, as there was little to be done until the next steps in the political maneuvering began to unfold. At the moment, the world was in a stalemate. Everyone else was gathered around the *messengers*.

"Oh, there you are!" said Alius. "It's about time you got here!"

"Where's the crew from the Island of the Children?"

"Oh, they're meeting with everyone down at the beach to help set the first pilings. With this fog, I'm sure they've enough to deal with today."

"What's happening here?"

"Well, we've been watching another speech by the Dark Lord. He's so charming, when he's not being demonic!"

"Anything new?"

"Not really, just rehashing their demands, riots and protests at foreign military posts and embassies in almost every Coalition country, and virtually no response from any of the industrial powers," said the Professor quietly.

"That doesn't really surprise me. What are they going to say?"

"You do have a point, young man."

One of the *messengers* buzzed and Ester turned to check it. "Alius, there seems to be an Internet message for you!"

Alius walked over to the glowing *orb* and smiled, "It's from Suzanne. Remember the lady with the baby in New York?"

Adrian smiled, "Yes, I do. She was really brave and her baby had our blue eyes!"

The little blond *seer* read the message in silence, reaching out to drag Adrian to the screen.

The message read, "**Dear Alius, you told me that, if I ever needed to get in touch with you, I could find you through the Internet. I must talk with you as soon as possible about a very private matter. Please respond at your earliest convenience. Love, Suzanne.**"

Alius hit reply and typed, "**Lovely to hear from you, how's Tiffin?**"

Within moments a reply flashed on the screen, "**Oh, he's growing so fast. I think you might want to see him, when you have time. I don't know but maybe your premonition about him was true. He's not like other children his age.**"

"**I'll make a point of it. Where are you?**"

"I'm living in Toronto now. I have a job and an apartment and I certainly have you to thank."

"I'm happy that things are better for you."

"Do you remember the Canadian gentleman who offered to help me?"

"Yes, I do."

"He suggested that I get in touch to see whether Adrian might contact him. I'm afraid he insisted that this is an emergency."

"What's his name and how would he be contacted?"

"His name is Lord Anthony Robbins. He's at his office in New York. 212-555-1000. Please ask Adrian to call him at once! Thanks, I love you! Suzanne."

"I'll see what I can do and I'll get back to you when there's time. Meantime, take care of that beautiful child!"

The two *seers* stared at each other. "I wonder what this is about?"

Alius leaned close, "We'll never know unless you call him. Maybe it has something to do with all the craziness in the world!"

Adrian stepped up to the *messenger* and said, "212-555-1000"

A moment later, a voice answered, "Canadian consulate. How may I direct your all?"

"I would like to speak with Lord Anthony Robbins, please."

"Who should I say is calling?"

Adrian paused. "My name is Adrian and I was asked to call him."

"Let me see if Lord Robbins is available," replied the receptionist curtly.

There was silence for almost a minute, followed by several clicks and a deep voice, "Is this the young man that I met in the United Nations General Assembly several months ago?"

"Yes, it is."

"I've been asked by a very important person to see whether I might arrange a meeting."

"Do I know this person?"

"Yes, you are aware of him, although I doubt you've ever met."

"Why does anyone of that stature want to speak with me?"

"I believe that you and you alone might offer some insight into the current dilemma that is gripping the globe."

Adrian hesitated for a moment, "This person wants to know about the spokesman for the New Coalition. What makes you think that I'm not part of that group?"

"I saw your rather amazing performance and I believe it offered evidence of your character."

"How would I get in touch with this very important person?"

"He could send transportation for you."

"I have no need for transportation and I honestly would rather not endanger my friends and family."

"I understand your concern. Perhaps I could give you an email address that would allow you to correspond in complete privacy."

"Let's start with that," replied Adrian.

"Type in the word POTUS...all capitals."

"Who is this person?"

"The address is an acronym."

All of a sudden, it dawned on Adrian, who whispered, "President of the United States."

Alius grasped his arm and giggled.

"I'll send him a message."

"Thank you. I think that everyone in the world might benefit from your conversation with this person."

"We'll see. Oh, and thank you for taking care of our friend Suzanne and her baby."

"It is my pleasure."

The line went dead and Adrian typed in the address that he had been given, along with the message, "I understand that you would like to have a conversation."

There was no response for several minutes. The news media made a joke of the president's lack of technical savvy and stories appeared in the newspapers and on television poking fun at him.

Presently, a line appeared on the screen. "You will have to forgive me. I am not particularly proficient with these machines. If you are who I believe you to be, then yes, I would very much like to talk with you at your earliest convenience."

"How would we accomplish that?"

"I could send transportation."

"If you are familiar with me, then you know that I won't need those arrangements."

"The only thing I know about you is what I've seen on the television but I understand your concern for...security."

"I think, under the circumstances, it has more to do with protecting the people who mean the most to me."

"I understand. There is a rose garden just outside my office. I will inform the guards that you will be arriving in a...rather unusual fashion."

Alius leaned over and whispered, "Do you realize who you are talking to?"

"Yeah."

"I want to go with you."

"Okay."

"I'll be traveling with a companion."

"I'll make the arrangements. When should we expect you?"

"We'll be there within the hour."

"Thank you."

Ester stifled a long sigh behind a fist firmly planted against her lips, "I don't believe this!"

Ponte just laughed, pushing his glasses up the bridge of his nose. "As I've said before...there is always more to learn and the Powers certainly work in mysterious ways."

Nanchez patted Adrian on the back, "So you're off for tea with the president, eh? Don't let it go to your head!"

Adrian laughed, "You know me better than that and, anyway, maybe we can help."

"Oh, I'm sure that you can help. It's just a matter of who's expecting what out of this meeting."

Ponte interrupted, "There's an old saying about the enemy of my enemy is my friend. That's not always the case but allying yourself...all of us for that matter, with one side or the other might be a dangerous undertaking."

The young *seer* stared at the floor, "I don't think that we have to ally ourselves with anyone. It always comes back to defending the Light and the Balance and doing the things that we know are right."

"Well, at least we can be sure that someone around here has their head on straight!" laughed Ester.

Nanchez glared, "Just understand, boy, that you'll be talking to the most powerful man in the world. He has his own agenda and his own purposes. There's as much to lose as there is to gain. This should be handled delicately and I wish that one of us could go with you. Take Mary or the Professor!"

"I'm taking Alius because we know we can count on each other and besides, there's a certain...I don't know, advantage to being considered children. He doesn't know our level of sophistication or, for that matter, our powers."

Ponte said, "I think I have to agree with the young people. They've shown great maturity in the missions they've undertaken and I have every faith in their ability to communicate with adults. The president asked Adrian to come for a chat...not you, not me, not anyone else. If he feels more comfortable taking Alius, then so be it!"

Adrian looked at Alius, who was wearing her robes, and then down at his jeans. Do you think that I could borrow robes from Raffe?"

Ester bustled through the dining room and into the bedroom wing. A few minutes later, she appeared with blue robes that looked almost new. "These might be a little large, but they'll do, although you really ought to be wearing a coat and tie!"

The young *seer* grabbed the robes, kissed Ester on the cheek, and disappeared down the hallway from which she just emerged. A minute later, he was back. "The sleeves are a little long and the hem at the bottom just barely scrapes the ground when I walk. I guess I'll just have to be tall!"

"I'd say that you're about to grow into them," laughed Ponte, "but not in time!"

Adrian walked over to Alius and took her hand, "You've been to Washington, so you should know your way around!"

"I only went to one very specific place and it was really scary!"

"I'm just teasing. I don't think that it'll be too hard to find and I'd be willing to bet that there is a vector originating from that house."

"I'll bet you're right," smiled the blond *seer*. "Shall we go?"

The Professor patted Alius on the back, "Just find the Lincoln Memorial on the Potomac, go east to the Washington Monument, then north to the White House."

"Thanks!"

The two *seers* kissed Ester and hugged Ponte and Nanchez, joined hands, and walked out the door into cool mist rolling across the island. Adrian leaned over to Alius and whispered, "One for all and all for one!"

A moment later, they were gone.

~

The *seers* clutched hands, as they zipped through the vectors. The smooth tones hummed without a trace of the grating sound of the dark vectors, although they were both aware that they could be intercepted at any time.

Adrian looked at Alius, "We know they're monitoring our movements, just as the Keepers monitor theirs, but I wonder whether they can tell who's moving along the vectors?"

"We did our best to foul up their systems to prevent them from connecting all the dark vectors but, at this point, there's really nothing that we can do about that anymore. We have to do what we must and we'll deal with each crisis as it arises."

"You're always right. There's no point in worrying about it but it is a curiosity and we ought to ask the Professor and Nanchez about that when we get back."

"I agree. I think we're almost there. Are you ready for this?"

"It's funny but, after all that we've been through, I'm not even nervous."

"I'm pretty sure I would be, if I weren't with you."

"Hold my hand and we'll be fine."

They flew over the Lincoln Memorial and the long reflecting pools, swept around the obelisk, and landed on a lush green lawn, surrounded by magnificent rose bushes budding in pinks, reds, and soft yellows. Instantly, four secret service agents appeared, hands on the guns beneath their coats, and one of them moved to frisk Adrian.

A voice called out with quiet assurance, "That won't be necessary, gentlemen. These children are my guests."

Adrian and Alius turned to greet the man who had spoken. They had only seen his photograph and clips of him on news broadcasts. He was shorter than they might have imaged but there was unyielding strength and intensity in his dark eyes and no doubt about who was in charge in this house.

"Please come into my office. May I offer you something?"

"Water would be fine," replied Alius.

"I'm afraid that I don't really know your names."

"I'm Adrian and this is my friend Alius."

"Do you have last names?"

"Everyone knows us as Adrian and Alius."

"Then I guess that will have to do. I certainly appreciate your coming to talk with me on such short notice but I assume you're aware of the events that are unfolding around the world."

"We are."

"What can you tell me about this man, Palloze?"

"There are some things that you must understand before you can appreciate how evil this man really is, let alone his true intentions."

"That's an interesting point of view from someone as young as you are," replied the president.

"I think that we would be wise to let my age be the subject of a future conversation," replied Adrian.

A guard opened the door and the children hesitated, waiting for the president to enter. He stopped and held out his hand for them to go before him, "Come on children, it is my prerogative to allow you to go first. You are children and you are my guests."

Adrian and Alius walked into an oval room, painted a light mustard yellow with white trim. An imposing desk sat between large windows, with a very large chair, and a blue carpet with the presidential seal covered the floor. There were formal portraits of past presidents hanging on the walls and a collection of family photos on a credenza against the wall.

The president walked behind his desk and tapped the intercom. "Natalie, could we please have three glasses of ice water?"

He gestured across the room to a facing pair of couches in front of a fireplace that warmed the room with its flickering flames. The children sat on one couch and the president on the other. He leaned forward, elbows on his knees, and stared at the two *seers* for almost a minute.

There was a knock at the door and a lady in a dark gray business suit walked into the room, carrying a tray with three glasses of ice water, which she offered to the president and the two children. "Will there be anything else, Sir?"

President Bartlett glanced at the two children, "No, I don't think that we'll be needing anything else. Thank you."

Adrian and Alius said, "Thank you," in unison.

"I honestly don't know how to approach this. I look at the two of you and I see two children but something tells me that my first impression is anything but complete. After reviewing your siege of the General Assembly, I was amazed to see you fly through the air. People don't fly through the air, at least not to my knowledge. Of course, today you just materialized on the lawn outside…no one I know does that either…and then there's your relationship with the animals. Towards the end of the tape that I watched of your…performance at the United Nations, you put your fingers in your mouth and whistled. Every animal in the room stopped whatever they were doing and turned to you. You gave them instructions, in common English, and they understood and obeyed. I find that astonishing."

Adrian blushed and Alius giggled. "The animals are our allies and our friends. In the place we come from, the humans and the animals work together on all levels. They help us and we help them. We call it the Balance and it applies to every facet of life. As to my instructing them, all of those animals had been discarded by their masters in the sewers of New York. They volunteered to help rescue our friend, Raffe, who'd been kidnapped by the man that you know as Palloze. Don't you think that we humans are sort of…arrogant, when it comes to showing respect for the animals? We have language, why do we suppose that they don't, just because we don't understand what they're saying? They certainly have no trouble understanding what we're saying."

"I guess you do have a point, I have a retriever who knows exactly what I want her to do before I say a word." He paused, "Your introduction changed the human attitude toward the animal world. Now, they're represented in the United Nations and there are programs around the world to promote a real understanding between the species."

"That is as it should be. Mr. President, there's another parallel world that's existed since time began. Actually, there are several. There's one that's the home of every animal that has ever lived. No humans are allowed to live there. It's a perfect animal world."

The president stared at the boy, unsure of what he was really saying. "Explain what you mean."

"There is a world that no one can see, yet it exists in the same time and the same space as what we call reality. Reality is really just one dimension of many," said Alius.

Adrian continued, "We traveled here on vectors that emanate from a series of giant crystals that exist in many places across the globe. The Crystals almost always come in pairs, one positive and the other negative. As it was explained to me, over the course of history you can identify civilizations that tapped into the power of the Crystals and matured at an incredible rate. Atlantis, China, Egypt, the tribes of Central and South America, Babylon…there are countless others. In the same way, you can find societies that found and used the Black Crystals, Hitler and Nazi Germany being an obvious example.

There are people today who are defending the Golden Crystals and all they stand for. There's also a mighty legion that we know as Legio Obscurum, an unseen army with incredible powers and a single purpose, controlling all of the Crystals and all of the Powers on the planet. They have people integrated into every government, every military, every intelligence agency, every religious organization, every financial institution, and, certainly, every media company. Wherever there's an opportunity to influence those in power or to move public opinion to accept their message, you'll find their people."

"How do you know this?"

Adrian stared at the president for a moment and then turned to look at Alius, who had a look in her eyes that insisted he be careful what he divulged. He turned back to the president and pulled up the hem of his robes to reveal the scars on his leg. "I earned these in a battle with the Dark Lord, Zepallo…or Palloze, as you know him."

The president stared at the burns until Adrian dropped his robe. "How could someone, as young as you are, do battle with a fully grown man who is, obviously, physically powerful?"

"He's a Master *Seer*. I'm only a novice but I'm faster and more creative than he is, so, in our last battle, I was lucky enough to strike the final blow."

"I don't think it had anything to do with luck. You used the term Master *Seer*, what is a *seer*?"

The two *seers* exchanged knowing glances, before Alius replied, "A *seer* is someone who can read from the ancient texts that have been handed down through the generations since the island of Atlantis was destroyed by a volcano. We've learned to use the Powers of the Crystals to do seemingly impossible things, like levitating or flying through the vectors."

Adrian added, "*Seers* are very rare, our abilities are inherited through our mothers in a lineage that goes back for thousands of years."

"I am humbled by my lack of knowledge."

"There's no reason that you would know about any of these things," said Alius. "Adrian didn't know that he was a *seer* until about a year ago."

"Yet, you've learned to fight successfully against this villain, Zepallo? Tell me, how was this battle waged?"

"I was armed with a sword, a shield, and a blaster ring, which fires an energy charge." He held up his hand to display the ring on his finger. "Zepallo used a similar ring to fire charges at us, while we were in the General Assembly. In our battle, he was armed with a crystal sword that was, not only, sharp but also a more powerful version of these rings."

Alius interrupted, "The fight occurred several hundred feet in the air, in the middle of a raging thunderstorm, and it lasted for, what seemed, a very long time."

"I'm impressed, although I have to admit that I want to be skeptical. So, you're telling me that there are multiple realities and secret armies? You'll have to admit, that is a bit hard to believe?"

"Mr. President, you invited us to come here to talk with you about the man who is leading the New Coalition. That's what we're trying to do. We have no reason to make up stories and the things that we're telling you have been known to our people for thousands of years," said Alius, curtly.

"I apologize," smiled President Bartlett. "I appreciate the fact that you came here to teach me about these things and I should have no reason not to believe what you are telling me."

Adrian burst out laughing, "Adults. They get stuck believing what they've been taught all their lives. We're no different than you, we've just learned different things about a world that exists along side the world that you live in. It's always been there and it will be there long after we humans have died off. It's real, it's beautiful...and the Crystals are more powerful than any other energy on the planet!"

Alius added, "We've been in the lairs of the Dark Forces. They monitor your military, your secret communications, and every diplomatic correspondence. They know everything that every government is doing or is intending to do. That is the truth."

The president's jaw dropped open. "Where are these 'lairs'?"

"We destroyed one of them and pretty well ruined two others. Do you remember that island in the Southern Atlantic that blew up for no reason last year?"

"Yes, I do remember seeing something about that."

"And the fires in the tunnels beneath Central Park in New York?"

"Yes."

"And a lake in the Caucus Mountains that drained itself for no reason?"

"Yes."

The two children stared at the president with mischief in their eyes.

"That was you two?"

"Well, there were a lot of people and animals who helped," replied Alius.

"They have centers all over the globe and their technology is expanding all the time. We've ruined three of them but that hasn't put them out of business. They just move to another one someplace else," added Adrian.

"Okay, tell me about this Palloze guy. What's his story?"

The two *seers* glanced at each other, before Alius began, "We don't know much about his history, although we've been told that he was a priest at the Vatican and overseer of their Crystals…and, yes, there are a pair of Crystals under the Holy City. It was rumored that he was being groomed to become the Pope someday, but, one day, he vanished without a trace."

"We first encountered him, when his people were trying to connect the vectors between all the Black Crystals in the World. If they had completed their network, there would have been no other power on Earth to resist their dominance. They would have controlled everything…every power source, the means of communication, anything that produced or consumed electricity…they could control it all. That was the island in the Southern Atlantic."

"He tried it again from the cavern in New York. This time, our Keepers tell us they aren't seeing anything unusual in the dark vectors." Adrian stopped and turned to Alius, "They've found another way."

Alius gasped, "It's so obvious! Why didn't we see it?"

The president looked confused. "What are Keepers?"

"They're our scientists and wise men," said Alius. "We've told you a little about the vectors and how we use them for energy, transportation, and communications. By tapping into the dark vectors, they could communicate with, say, the leaders of each of the Coalition countries and you'd never know, because it wouldn't be carried on any wavelength that your scientists are aware of. It would be invisible. Zepallo can pop up in any capitol in the world and disappear just as easily."

All of a sudden, the president's eyes focused sharply. "I'm beginning to see what you've been trying to tell me. This is incredible. Do we have Crystals?"

Alius giggled, "Yes, Sir, you do."

"Where do we keep them?"

"There's a pair under the Lincoln Memorial. I've seen them."

The president stopped and stared at the young girl. "And how is it possible that a young girl, from who knows where, has seen these Crystals and I, the President of the United States, didn't even know they existed?"

"It's a long story, Mr. President. But, if you don't believe me, there must be a security tape somewhere of a confrontation that happened last summer, where the police were called to the Memorial to investigate a girl who had emerged from a secret opening behind the statue. I was that girl."

"That's incredible!"

"Well, not really. Adrian had a couple of really weird encounters on that mission and our friend, Raffe, had one with giant slugs and another with thousands of skeletons. We've had to do some strange stuff over the past year to keep Zepallo from succeeding."

"Sometime, we'll have to talk about your adventures but you still haven't told me about the guy!"

"Oh, him?" giggled the children. "Okay, until a few months ago, there was a council of Master *Seers* for the Dark Forces, called the Council of Ollapez. Zepallo, a relatively young but powerful and brilliant wannabe, was held in check by several older *seers* and Keepers. Unfortunately, in the battle that we told you about, we sank their command submarine and the elder *seers* went down with it, which allowed Zepallo to seize control of the Council and Legio Obscurum.

He's the only truly evil person that I've ever met. He has no concept of the value of life and he'll stop at nothing to get what he really wants."

"What is it that he wants?"

Adrian stared at the floor for a long moment, "To rule the world."

"Well, he's certainly on his way to accomplishing that goal. Is there any way to stop him?"

"Using your forces, no," replied Adrian. "If you could catch him and put him in jail, he'd just move through the vectors and appear somewhere else. You couldn't hold him and I doubt that you could kill him, he's far too powerful and skilled to fall to any normal human. Only a *seer* could do battle with him and have any chance of surviving, let alone winning."

"And he's only been defeated by one person," said Alius quietly, glancing at Adrian.

"There's no other way?" asked President Bartlett in frustration.

"I think there might be another way," said Adrian quietly. "We have to convince the people of the world that it's time for everyone to stop being afraid of each other. It's time for all of us to come together as one people, helping and caring for each other, protecting the animals, and giving back to the Earth that supports us. If everyone believed that…truly believed that…then there would be no need for the New Coalition…or NATO…or any formal alliance…or governments for that matter. We could all just be citizens of the world."

The president sat back in his seat and stared at Adrian, "Do you realize what the people of the world would think, what the media would print, and television newscasters would say, if I gave a speech saying those things? They'd laugh me out of office!"

"You couldn't say them…but I could," said Adrian quietly.

Chapter 10

Sara, Elsie, Mrs. Green, Mrs. Stevens, and several other ladies were busy in the back room of the apothecary, sewing diving suits from the materials that had been supplied by their friends from the Island of the Children.

Every once in a while, small groups of Islanders wandered in to be scanned. One by one, they slipped behind a screen, disrobed, and stood in the middle of the round vertical tube.

One of the women would ask, "Are you ready?"

The subject would respond, "Yes."

"Now stand up very straight, close your eyes, and hold your arms down at your sides. These suits need to fit like a glove, so be very still."

Mashing a button on a console caused a flash of white light to whirl around the person in the tube. A moment later, the process was complete and their exact measurements recorded and transferred to a machine that cut all the panels to be fitted together.

The first batch of suits was ready to be delivered and Soule and Amy were ready to start their first classes with the eager students. The reaction would be the same for everyone on the island as it had been for those who returned from the mission to the Island of the Children. Every novice would want to go again, although they would all be completely exhausted after their first dive.

Elsie glanced at the tiny *orb* on her wrist, "Oh my, I must be going. Everyone will be needing some dinner."

Sara looked up for her sewing machine, "I'm just about finished with this one but there are so many left to do!"

Nancy Smith looked up at Elsie, "I could give you a ride back to the House of Four Seasons, if you'd like, then Sara could finish her work here."

"That would be lovely, dear, if you don't mind."

"I don't mind at all, it's right on the way."

Elsie turned to Sara, "Why don't I go on and get things started at the house and you can finish up here. There's no need to hurry."

Sara smiled, "I'll just finish one more and then I'll catch up with you. Adrian promised to be back in time for dinner tonight."

"There's much too much going on right now. The whole island is buzzing with activity!"

Elsie and Nancy gathered their things and hugged their friends before heading off.

Sara bent over her machine and continued sewing. One by one, the other ladies excused themselves and she was left alone. An hour later, she finished and decided that she had accomplished enough for one day. There was always tomorrow but there were still hundreds of suits to be made.

She draped her shawl around her shoulders and stepped to the door, where she said, "Good night!" All the *orbs* dimmed and she walked out to the trolley, which was parked on the quay. A wispy fog rolled over calm water in the little bay and up through the village. It was cold and damp, so she gathered her wrap and climbed into the cab of the old trolley, pushed the starter button, and stepped on the accelerator. It moved off up the hill, out of the little village, and onto the plain.

The last rays of sunset sparkled over the ridge, so she turned on the *orbs* to light the path ahead. She was pleased with the progress they were making and excited at the chance to dive again. It would be fun to go with Adrian and his friends and she was looking forward to helping with the construction of the domes. Life on the island was about to change for the better. They might not have more land but they would have access to the wonders and bounties of the sea.

Up ahead, she noticed a dark form in the fog at the side of the road. At first, she thought it might be an old tree trunk but she never noticed it before. The trolley slowed, as she approached the mysterious shape.

Suddenly, it moved into the middle of the path, directly in front of her, and unfurled what appeared to be branches, which stretched out like the wings of a giant bat. A black cape billowed behind the large figure and the mist swirled in the light of the *orbs* on the front of the trolley. She lifted her foot off the accelerator and the trolley came to a stop within a few feet of the dark mirage. She could see a white face staring from beneath a dark hood, a sinister smile curled at the corners of thin lips beneath electric blue eyes. She recognized that face. She had seen it when she and Adrian visited their old house on the bay and been confronted by Zepallo.

Before she could reverse or steer around him, the Dark Lord was leaning on the front of the trolley. He flipped back the cowl that covered most of his face to reveal a broad smile, "I'm so happy to see you, my dear. I so hoped that you'd be coming this way."

Sara leaned out of the trolley, "What do you want?"

"I thought that it might be a nice opportunity for us to have a little chat."

"I have nothing to say to you," replied Sara. Her hands were shaking but she was trying desperately to maintain calm in her voice.

"That's too bad, because we'll be spending some time together."

"What do you mean?" She looked around but there was no one within miles who might help and the fog limited visibility to almost nothing.

"I think your son will be inclined to behave in a much more civilized manner, if you're with me. There are important things happening in the world and I don't want to have to worry about interference from Adrian. You will be my insurance."

"Not willingly!" screamed Sara, pushed back hard on the foot pedal, throwing the trolley into reverse.

Zepallo reached a pale hand and seized the front of the truck. Sara twisted the wheel and pushed the throttle forward but the spinning wheels kicked up a cloud of dust and the trolley did not move. "My dear, there's no point in ruining this lovely vehicle. Neither you nor it are going to escape me, so why don't you just relax and come along peacefully?"

"There's nothing peaceful about you!"

"There's no need for violence. I'm simply asking you to accompany me on a short journey, where you will be well cared for, I promise!"

"Your promises mean nothing."

"That may be true, but, in this case, maintaining your well-being is to my advantage. Now come along."

The Dark Lord moved around to the side of the trolley and reached in to grab Sara's arm. He lifted her out of her seat and placed her on the ground. "You will find that I am a gracious host."

"I want nothing to do with you, now go away and leave me alone!"

"My dear, we have so much to talk about!" He drew his crystal sword from a sheath on his belt and pointed it at the side of the trolley. "Don't you think an emblem would add some class to this...vehicle?"

A short bright blast hit the side of the old trolley. A small puff of smoke evaporated into the haze, revealing an ornate golden 'Z' less than two inches tall etched into the panel.

Zepallo smiled, returned the sword to its sheath, and placed his hand on her shoulder. "You might call it my personal message to your son. Just so there is no doubt about your whereabouts. We don't want to worry your family!"

A moment later, they moved into the dark vectors. Sara covered her ears against the high-pitched grating and felt as if she was being dragged through the heart of a massive thunderstorm. Inky black clouds churned and licks of lightning raced through the sky, thunder cracked and rumbled and, in the depths of her soul, she was sure that she would not live to see her son or her husband again.

The tall *seer* just smiled and, within a few minutes, they landed at the mouth of a large cave, where a bitterly cold wind charged down a craggy snow covered mountain. Sara had no idea where they were but she was sure that it was far from Morgan's Knot and she was scared. Zepallo held her arm firmly, as he escorted her past two saluting guards into the mouth of a long cavern, which pulsed with purple lights rippling along an endless corridor.

~

Adrian couldn't wait to tell his mother about meeting with the president, let alone that he decided to arrange for the young *seer* to speak before the United Nations.

Alius was almost serene as they whizzed through the vectors. She had been a grounding voice, during their conversation in the Oval Office, explaining background and adding depth. Adrian doubted that the president would have believed him, if he had been alone.

He thought about his conversation with his older self and suddenly understood that he had not been given a progression of events that would lead to the things they had talked about. This speech was the beginning but that strange chill clawed up his spine and exploded at back of his skull, followed by the loud grating of the dark energies interrupting the smooth tones of the golden vectors and dimming the flowing colors. It only lasted for a moment but rattled the young *seers* out of their thoughts.

Alius grabbed his robes and pulled him close, "What was that?"

"I don't know but I just had one of those hedaches again. Something bad has happened."

The giddiness and excitement thawed and she could see the depth of feeling, the torment in his eyes. She sensed the pain of the whole world run through his body and, for the first time, saw that he was taking in things far beyond his immediate surroundings. In that moment, she was overwhelmed by the sheer weight and mass of it, a duty he could not carry through life alone.

"I'm with you until we're finished," she whispered.

"I have a feeling that whatever is happening will be far beyond anything we've had to deal with before."

"I don't care. That's all the more reason why you can't do this alone. We're both stronger when we're together. Add Simian, Mary, Sky, Master Chi, and the others and we're the only force who can stand against the Darkness. The president got part of it but there's no way that he can really understand the potential of the Dark Forces. He has nothing to reference it to…except the tales of a couple of kids. Even if we are special."

"I know. I wanted to be honest with him but it didn't take long to understand that he can't openly support us until there's some momentum. He's worried about politics and the survival of his nation as a superpower, instead of worrying about saving the world. No single nation can stand against the Dark Forces. Their spies are already buried in governments and all the rest. He didn't want to believe that and, besides, if the people of the world hear our message, he'll be out of a job."

"I know but, at least, he's willing to let you tell the story and that's a start. What are you going to say?"

"I know the theme…Fear! I just don't quite know how I'll explain it. I guess it will come to me before I get there."

"The president said that he'd ask Lord Robbins to arrange for you to speak tomorrow."

Adrian's lips rose into a weak grin, "Then I'd better start thinking about it!"

The moon peeked through misty clouds with a soft, eerie radiance lighting the path, as they landed outside the observatory. The lights inside were glowing through the front door, which was standing open. Ester always insisted that the door be kept closed, "It's only proper!"

The two *seers* walked up the steps, through the foyer, and into the parlor, but there was no one there. They could feel that the house was empty and knew that something was terribly wrong.

From the porch, they noticed the flash of *orbs* on the path to the village, in the distance. They joined hands and tried to settle themselves enough to levitate. Adrian took Alius' other hand and looked directly into her eyes, "We must be calm. We must be sure. We'll move as one."

They took off across the fields, soaring through the night to several silhouettes moving around in the headlights of a vehicle. Alius said, "It's the trolley and there's Travis' old truck and the Professor's wagon."

Ester was the first to spot them landing next to the old wagon, "I'm so glad you're here."

Adrian raced around the car, where Ponte and Travis were inspecting the side panel. A very formal "Z" was etched into the metal. The Professor put an arm around Adrian, "Your mother is missing. Travis found the trolley here and there's no sign of her."

"He's taken her!" screamed Adrian, crumbling to his knees. His head fell forward to touch the ground and he melted into a puddle of blue robes. Before Alius could reach out to console him, he hissed, "I'll kill him and I'll get her back!"

The mist whirled and the imprint, where his knees, toes, and forehead had touched the path, was the only evidence that he had been there.

"Oh, my..." whispered Ester. "Where did he go?"

Alius looked up at her, "He's gone to find a dark vector and there's only one place on the island where he can gain access. It's in the mountain and I have to go after him!"

The Professor touched her shoulder with a firm but gentle hand. His voice was quiet but stern, "We have one *seer* who is out of control, let's not have two. You must catch up with him and convince him to give us a little time to do some research and investigation. We can review the monitors to see where the disruptions occurred and where they lead. If he goes off on his own, it will surely be the death of both of them."

"I know you're right," sighed the blond *seer*, "but, if I am to catch him, I must hurry!"

"Then go!" replied Ponte. "If you find him, take him back to the House of the Four Seasons. His father will need him as much as he'll need John. I'll call you when we have something to work with."

Alius closed her eyes and concentrated on the chamber that held the Black Crystal in the mountain. A moment later, she vanished.

Within seconds, she was standing before the giant black gem, which was spinning at a dizzying rate. A high pitched grating whine clattered around the cavern and she found Adrian standing before the Crystal, his arms in the air, frantic eyes wild and desperate, and he was chanting, "I am willing, I am able, I will kill to save her...show me the way!"

Alius ran up behind him and wrapped her arms around his chest. "You can't do this!"

"I have no choice, I have to save her!"

"If you find your way into the Dark plane, you won't save her life. Don't you see, this is exactly what Zepallo wants you to do, he wants you to walk right into his trap and, this time, there'll be no escape!"

Adrian spun around and pushed Alius to the floor, "You can't stop me. I'm far more powerful than you will ever be! It's not your mother he's taken, it's mine!"

Alius just stared at her friend for a moment. A tear rolled down her cheek, "In all the world, you have no better friend than I have been to you and you never will. As I said earlier, you can't do this alone and you know that we're both stronger when we're together. When the time is right, I'll help you in any way I can...but this is not the time. This is a trap that a foolish young *seer* would fall into without thinking, without preparing, and it will be death for you, your mother, and everything that we stand for...is that what you really want?"

Adrian stood absolutely still, his arms in the air, his fists clenched tight, and screamed with a ferocity that Alius had never heard before. It was a death cry, ripped from someplace deep in his soul, filled with hate, fury, and excruciating pain, the sound of young boy's heart breaking.

The roar echoed around the chamber, reverberating and multiplying, growing in intensity, until it finally faded into the hissing gale whirling around the chamber. Alius sat up and held out her hand to Adrian, who slowly slumped to his knees before her. Sobbing, he fell forward and buried his face in her stomach.

She wrapped her arms around him, "The time will come, but it's not now...you're not ready and we both know that Zepallo is waiting for you. Killing you would clear the way for everything he wants. There's another way, a better way."

Adrian sobbed, "I have to save her."

"You'll have the chance but let's do this the right way."

He did not respond but held her tight.

"The Professor said that he'd go back to the observatory and review the monitors to see where the disruptions were and where Zepallo might have taken her. In the meantime, your father needs you."

Adrian sat up. "Father?"

"Don't you think he's worried too? She's his wife and the mother of his child. Losing one of you would be bad enough, losing both of you...?"

"I have to go to him," sighed Adrian.

"I'll take you."

~

Travis and Ester arrived in time to inform the family of Sara's disappearance. Elsie and Ester were waiting at the top of the kitchen steps, when the two *seers* arrived. Adrian was sobbing and the two women took him in their arms.

Elsie said, "It wasn't that long ago that Ester was kidnapped and we managed to get her back. I know that we'll find a way to retrieve your mother. You just have to believe."

Adrian looked into her blue eyes, the tears rolling down his cheeks, "Don't you see, he's taken her as leverage against me. I'm the only one who stands in his way and, now, anything I do will endanger her life. Checkmate."

They held each other for a long time, as friends slowly crowded into the kitchen to console the rest of the family. Finally, his aunt whispered, "Does this remind you of anything?"

Adrian remembered their conversation before he climbed the mountain to replace the balancing crystal. "Yes."

"I think we both learned a valuable lesson from that experience. Perhaps, this is the time to put that knowledge to work."

"I...I...don't know what I can do..."

"You can be the *seer* that your mother is so proud of...and you can be the person that you know, in your heart, you are. I believe that we'll find a way to get her back. We just have to trust in each other and in the Power of the Light. Every problem that you've faced has offered a solution...perhaps not the obvious one but...somehow, you found a way to the right path. You can and will do it again."

Adrian's legs were weak. He felt as if all the strength and confidence had been drained from his body. He leaned on his aunt, as they turned into the kitchen.

His father was waiting just inside the door and enveloped his son. There was a sense of safety in his embrace but Adrian could feel his father's uneven breathing and warm tears falling on his hair, dripping down his face to mix with his own.

John guided Adrian into the living room, everyone else stayed behind, understanding that this was a private moment. They sat on the couch, in the darkness, and cried together.

Finally, his father pulled back and looked down at his son, "I don't have the magic that you inherited from your mother and, to tell you the truth, I find it rather intimidating to have a son who can do the things that you can do...but I am so very proud of you, of everything you've accomplished, and the person you've become."

Adrian could not respond, knowing that his father loved him and adored his wife, but they were never as close or as open with each other as he was with his mother.

"I have to admit that I'm completely terrified at the thought of your mother being held captive by that...villain...but I think we should consider this from her point of view. What would she tell you to do, under these circumstances?"

Adrian cuddled against his father's chest and thought about the question, "I think that we both know what she'd tell me to do."

John laughed quietly, "She'd tell you to do what you know you must, in spite of the danger to her. You know that she is so very proud of you."

"I know," whispered Adrian. "I want to fight. I want to go after him and destroy everything he stands for...that's what my heart is telling me."

"But that isn't the correct answer, is it?"

"No."

"You already know that this is a trap and he expects you to jump into it. Be patient. The answer will present itself when the time is right."

"I know but there's a part of me that wants to rush through the vectors to begin this battle. Alius was right. I'm not ready."

"No, but you will be..."

They were quiet for a while, finding comfort in each other.

"Where were you today? You've been gone for a long time."

"You probably wouldn't believe me if I told you."

"Yes, I would."

"I went to have a conversation with the President of the United States in the Oval Office."

His father laughed, "You did what?"

"Honest. He invited me to have a chat about Zepallo and the New Coalition. Alius went with me."

"Why did he want to talk with you?"

"Because of what we did in the United Nations."

"Ah, that makes sense, still…the President of the United States! I'll bet he doesn't invite too many children in to counsel him on world affairs."

"You're probably right."

"What did you tell him?"

"We tried to explain about the Crystals and the Powers, about the Dark Forces, and about Zepallo and his true intentions. I hope he believed some of it."

"What does he want you to do?"

"He's arranging for me to give a speech to the United Nations… tomorrow."

"Say that again…"

"You heard me."

"He wants a boy to stand up in front of the whole world and tell them the truth?"

Adrian smiled, "Alius and I were talking about that and we realized that if I tell the whole truth, he'll be out of a job."

"Does that qualify as cross-purposes?"

"I think it does."

"Are you going to do it?"

"It's weird…an hour ago, I was so excited, I couldn't stand it. Now, I'm afraid to do anything that might make things worse for Mom."

"And what would she say?"

"She would say that I should go and give a great speech. Tell the truth and nothing less."

"Then that's what you have to do."

Adrian laughed quietly, "It always comes down to doing what must be done…doing what is right and true."

"I think we've solved that problem. Now, all we have to do is to figure out where he's taken your mother and how to get her back."

"I'm not afraid of him but I am afraid of what he might do to her."

"I know…but if you don't try, if you don't move forward, then she is surely lost and he has won the ultimate battle…without having to face you."

Adrian looked into his father's eyes. For the first time, he felt that his father really understood and he curled up and cried quietly. Finally, he pulled back, "There's something I have to tell you."

"What's that?"

"While I was in training, I fell asleep and I had a dream that mother had fallen in love with Zepallo and the two of them were trying to convince me to join them to conquer the world."

His father's jaw dropped open, "So…what happened?"

"She said that you had given them your blessing. I couldn't and wouldn't give up all that I believe in, even if she was asking me. Finally, Zepallo held out his sword and touched the end of my nose and defied me to join him or die. I wanted to use my blaster ring but I couldn't get a clear shot without hitting mom too. It was a stalemate and then I woke up."

"And what do you think it meant?"

"At first, I realized that the dream was all about love. Love is the reason we do the things that we must and, at the same time, it's the one weakness we can't control. Does that make any sense?"

"Yes, it does. Love is the most precious thing that anyone can share with another, yet when it goes wrong, or when it's taken away, there's nothing that hurts more. I understand what you're saying and I think you're right. Unfortunately, it seems that your dream had a bit of premonition to it. The question is what can we do now?"

"The Professor's reviewing the monitors to follow the disruptions in the vectors. There's a trail there somewhere and it will lead to their lair. In the meantime, I have to give that speech tomorrow. The future of the world depends on it."

"That's the Adrian I know…the one that I'm so very proud of, the one who will find a solution to this problem, and the one who will bring his mother home safely." His father kissed him on the forehead, "I believe."

~

Adrian slept in his parents' bed that night. He just needed to be close to his father and the faint scent of his mother on the pillow soothed his anger and his fear.

He awoke with a start, to find George leaning over him, "The Professor's on the *messenger* and there's an email from a Lord Robbins."

His father rolled over, "It's going to be a big day for you. Before you start, I want you to know how much I love you and how proud I am of the person that you are. I believe in you absolutely and know that you...or we...will find a way to rescue your mother. When you find yourself doubting, just remember that she believes in you too and she loves you more than anything in the world."

Adrian leaned over and hugged his dad, "Thanks! I'll do my best."

"That's all anyone could ask. Now get going!"

The young *seer* leapt out of the bed and was about to pull Raffe's blue robes over his head, when he looked across the room and noticed his own robes, neatly folded on the bureau. His mother had mended them before she left for the village.

Scampering down the stairs, he noticed the sun shining through the east windows. It was going to be a beautiful day on Morgan's Knot. He wondered what it was like, wherever his mother was being held.

The Professor looked tired and Adrian could see Ester, Nanchez, and Dadeus behind him. "Good morning my boy. How are you feeling?"

Adrian hesitated for a moment, "Sad, tired, and ready for a fight!"

"That's the spirit. We've been doing some research and think we've found a trail. Could you come by?"

"Yes, but I have to respond to a message first and I think that I'll have to give a speech today."

"Alius told us about your meeting yesterday. I'm not particularly political, but I am impressed."

"Well, thank you...but don't be. It always comes back to doing what we must."

The Professor smiled, "Somehow, doing what we must always seems to ask a bit more of you than anyone else."

"I know what you mean but there's really nothing that any of us can do about that. We have to work together to find solutions to rescuing my mother and to the bigger problem. I couldn't have accomplished any of the things that I've done, without you and Ester and Nanchez...and Alius. We're a team."

Ponte laughed quietly, "It's nice to be needed!"

"I'll see you in a little while. I have to respond to this message and find out what time I'm expected to speak. In the meantime, could you check the news and see what's happening in the world?"

"We'll see you in a little while."

The *orb* dimmed and the email tag appeared before the screen. Adrian tapped it and it read, **Dear Adrian. I spoke with our mutual friend who requested that I set up a time for you to speak today. There is an unscheduled slot at 3:00 this afternoon, local time. If you are willing, please let me know. Sincerely, Lord Robbins.**

Adrian typed, **"Dear Lord Robbins, things have become a bit more complicated but I appreciate your help in making these arrangements and I will be there at the time that you requested. Thank you, Adrian."**

The young *seer* turned from George's study into the kitchen and found the whole family sitting around the oval table. Elsie was serving breakfast and Adrian stomach rumbled.

The twins looked up with the saddest expressions. "We're so sorry about your mom," said Megan.

"Whatever we can do to help get her back, you know you can count on us!" added Molly.

"I don't have any idea of how we'll get her back, but we will. We just have to believe in each other."

Chapter 11

Adrian arrived at the observatory to find Simian, Sky, Master Chi, and Shambala along with Sammy, Raffe, Mary, Dadeus, Gabrielle, Nanchez, Ponte and Ester, and, of course, Alius, waiting in the parlor. He sensed the room had been brimming with chatter before he arrived and, now, everyone was staring at him with sad eyes and deep concern.

All at once, without a word, they surrounded the young *seer* in a giant hug. Sky whispered, "We're so sorry that your mother has been taken and we're here to find a way to bring her back. There is nothing that we would not do to help."

"I know and thank you," said Adrian quietly. "I'm afraid there are other things that must come first."

The Professor put an arm around his shoulders and led him into the dining room. On the table, Adrian spied an odd gray *orb* with several wires hooked to either end.

Ponte picked it up and handed it to Adrian. It was light and he wanted to toss it but resisted, holding it with both hands. "What's this?"

His mentor smiled, "I'm afraid that I am guilty of recording parts of the battle over Morgan's Knot. Those images are stored in this *orb*."

"What do you mean? You recorded the battle?"

"I mean exactly what I said!" stammered the old man. "Several of the Keepers are keen on making images through an interesting property that they've found in certain lavender crystals."

"You mean like recording a video on a tape or a disk?"

"Yes."

"What's on this…*orb*?"

"They set up remote crystals across the island which allowed us to see what was going on and the system recorded scenes of the initial invasion, the battles around the village, in the fields, at the House of the Four Seasons, at the entrance to the mountain and the observatory, and, of course, your duel with Zepallo. There are some interesting angles from the top of the mountain and along the ridge line."

"You mean you actually made a movie out of the invasion?"

"Well, it's more a documentary."

"I don't believe it!"

Master Chi spoke softly, "My young friend, don't you think the world might be interested in seeing this film before your speech?"

Adrian was dumbfounded and, honestly, did not know how to respond. He stared at the gray *orb* for a moment, "I'm not really sure that the world is ready to see what's on this video…"

Gabrielle interrupted, "The young man does have a point. There are some things that might better be kept as our secrets, for the time being. Telling the world about the dangers of the Dark Forces is one thing…actually showing them is quite another."

Sky followed the discussion moving from one person's opinion to another's and finally said, "I think Adrian is right. If he's going to talk to the people of the world, then his message must be one that they can embrace, one they can take into their hearts, and join together to change the political and economic balance. I don't think it's necessary or wise to give them something else to be afraid of…they'll have enough to think about already."

Simian smiled, "I knew that there was at least one more reason why I love you so much. There might well come a time when these images should be shown to the world…a time when they are ready, when they can truly understand what they're seeing. If they see it out of context, they might think that it's a promotion for one of those action movies, rather than the real life and death struggle it was. I agree with Sky, Adrian should speak from his heart about what he knows to be right and true. Anything more or less detracts from the beauty and simplicity of his message."

Everyone stared at the old Jamaican, perhaps in awe of his ability to sum up everyone's thoughts and arguments in such a beautiful way. "Well put," said Ponte. "I'll stash this away for safe keeping."

Dadeus stepped up to Adrian and held out a wooden box. The *seer* accepted it and opened the lid. Inside was the handle of the sword that Master Chi had given to him before the battle with Zepallo. He looked up at Dadeus, "I thought that I'd destroyed this."

"Well, it took a bit of doing, but I think that you'll like the improvements I've made. It's perfectly balanced and I've increased the range and power of the blaster a bit."

Adrian held it up before him and pressed the gemstone on the handle. A golden crystal blade slid from the grip, radiating an amber glow. The Keeper was right, the balance was perfect and he tipped it this way and that, before retracting the blade and bowing to Dadeus. "Thank you for repairing it."

"If you are to stand against the Dark Lord, then you should have a weapon to equal his," said the Keeper from the Island of the Children.

Adrian handed the sword to Master Chi, who inspected the workmanship with admiration and respect. Turning to Dadeus, he, too, bowed, "I'm impressed. We'll need more of these."

"I know," replied the Keeper. "My people are working on increasing production of a simpler version for the rest of the Light Forces, as well a hand cannon that will throw bundles of energy over longer distances with astonishing accuracy. After the last battle, we know that there will be other confrontations and we must be prepared."

Alius took Adrian's arm, "Do you know what you're going to say?"

Adrian placed the sword in an inside pocket of his robes, as he remembered the words of his older incarnation. "Yes, I think I do. It's all about fear…actually, it's about the choice between fear and love…"

No one spoke but everyone understood, for the message was the history and the common bond that drove these people to defend the Power of the Light and the wonder of the Positive Crystals. It was the balance of nature and the equilibrium that can exist only when man lives in harmony with his surroundings, instead of trying to dominate and manipulate the wonders nature has provided.

The Crystals offered more power than mankind might ever need, yet, through the energy of the Black Crystals, the Dark Forces always threatened the future. Adrian opened the first door of understanding for the world, when the animals converged on the United Nations. He was about to open a second and no one could possibly know whether the people of the world would understand the simple truth of his message.

The course of history was about to change and there were two possible outcomes to the crisis that was raging in the capitals of every nation. The first, and most obvious, was that the industrial powers and the New Coalition would bluff themselves into war, war that would provide Zepallo the opportunity to rule the remnants of civilization without firing a shot. The alternative seemed to include the dissolution of the political, economic, and religious foundations that ruled the world through the centuries. It was not that those institutions should be destroyed, rather it was time for the common people to take the future into their own hands. The real question would become a choice between the Light and the Dark.

Adrian would only get one chance to educate the people about the decision they had to make. A boy was about to take on the responsibility for the future of all mankind and he had never given a speech before a class, let alone the entire population of the world, well, other than their mission to rescue Raffe, which was spontaneous at best.

The elders in the room knew that Adrian had matured far beyond his years and possessed a keen ability to see through the chaos of the moment to the ultimate truth. They put great trust in his abilities, his instincts, and his discretion, yet, this time, there was another factor. No one could see what he was feeling in his heart but they all sensed the pain and fear that accompanied his mother's abduction, and each wondered whether he could focus on his mission with his usual precision.

Adrian could sense the distance that the elders were maintaining in the deference in their eyes and words filled with hesitant concern. It was time to turn the tables on them, "Alright, I've told you my basic idea for this talk. If each of you were in my position, what one thing would you add?"

Ponte was the first to speak, "I think that I would quote President Roosevelt, who said, 'The only thing that we have to fear is fear itself.'"

"Well put," said Gabrielle, "I think that I'd add that our greatest fears come from deep inside ourselves. The internal struggle is far more frightening than any enemy who might attack from without."

Master Chi added, "There's the inverse of that thought. Peace isn't something that we inhale or absorb from the outside, it grows from the soul. It's not only a state of mind but a state of being. That miraculous state is available to anyone who is willing to accept the responsibility for it."

Sky continued the idea, "My Master taught me to look at the destination rather than the path at my feet. Each of us is capable of achieving miraculous feats but they're only magical because we didn't believe ourselves capable in the first place. It is that belief that allows us to transcend our present to achieve our futures."

Alius smiled, "That was deep and beautiful. Perhaps the message should include the idea that the people of the world can empower themselves. They don't need the permission of a government or a religion or any higher authority. Each of us has the power and the responsibility to make the world better for everyone."

Sammy giggled, "I think that I'd quote the Beatles, "All you need is love!"

Ester laughed with him, "I don't think it can be put in more simple terms!"

"If I were you," said Raffe, "I think I'd mention something about the little man you met in the Vatican, the one who had lived in virtual isolation to protect the Crystals because he truly believed in what he was doing. Having that belief is power enough."

"That's very similar to what we teach our children," said Shambala. "If you truly believe that you can do something...say fly...you might not have the ability now, but your belief will drive you and lead you to find a way to make it real. Taking it to its finest level, belief is enough to create reality."

"Oooh, I love that," whispered Mary. "The texts tell us that each of the civilizations of our ancestors, those who found the Crystals and learned to use them to create a better world...each of those peoples maintained a simple lifestyle, a simple set of rules that they lived by, and a simple view of the future. The future included the betterment of all mankind, not just those who happened to believe as they believed. The bounty of their discoveries overflowed to benefit everyone around them and that's the way it should be in our world now."

"I treasure your thoughts and I'll try to use them in my speech," said Adrian quietly.

"Are you sure that you're ready for this?" inquired Mary. "The speech is one thing, the press and the questions are quite another."

"I didn't volunteer to speak to the press, I said that I would speak the truth to the world and that's what I'll do."

Master Chi said quietly, "I believe that you would be well served if the other *seers* accompanied you."

"The president asked me to speak."

"I know and I'm not suggesting that we do anything but act as representatives of the world that you are going to talk about. Our presence speaks for itself. Besides, you have to get from here to there. Zepallo has intercepted you and others who were traveling on the vectors, it's not beyond his capacity to try to silence you before you begin. At least, in our company, you'll have some protection."

Adrian started to say, "But..."

Alius interrupted, "The president didn't say anything that might restrict who accompanies you or appears on that stage. I agree with Master Chi, we're all going with you."

It was decided and Adrian gave in without argument. In a way, it would be comforting to have his friends in support of what he was about to do. There had not been time to feel nervous about speaking to a world forum but that queasy feeling in the pit of his stomach was testament to the rumblings in his subconscious. He was terrified about his mother and, if he had to admit it, he was feeling a bit of anticipation about the approach of his talk this afternoon. It was already past noon.

"What are your plans for your arrival?" asked Simian.

"I guess I thought that I'd just appear on the podium," replied Adrian.

"It might be more fun to fly around the room a few times before you land," suggested Raffe. "It certainly had an effect the last time you did it and it would show that you have powers equal to those of the Dark Lord."

Adrian smiled, "I like that!"

Sky added, "If we're going to fly around the room, then we should make it appear that it's a ballet...an aerial ballet!"

Alius giggled, "Maybe this time they might appreciate it if we didn't allow their chamber to be shot up with blasters!"

"Let's hope we have a receptive audience," said Simian. "A bit of fun at the beginning is fine, but this is serious business. The future of the world might depend, not only, on what you say but how it is received and interpreted."

"I agree," said Ponte. "Say what you have to say in the most gentle way that you can but with enough force to make it real. We know you but they don't and they're going to see a boy in blue robes who is hardly tall enough to speak into the microphone on the podium. If it's possible, pick up the mike and carry it off to one side, so they can see you."

"That's good theater," chortled Ester, as she wrapped an arm around Adrian. "I do think he has a point but my only advice to you, and perhaps the last bit of advice that you need to hear from this group, is to just be yourself. Speak clearly from your heart and they will understand."

Adrian leaned into her hug and smiled, "Thank you."

Chapter 12

The vectors seemed smooth, as the eight *seers* zipped along the paths to the United Nations building in New York City. Suddenly, there was a loud jangling and the fluid colors withered into molten shades of gray. A massive tangle of lightning sizzled around them and their motion slowed.

The *seers* turned to a hideous cry from the east, where a vision of Sara appeared with hundreds of snakes covering her body, writhing in a hideous pulsating rhythm. Her eyes blazed with terror, purple flames burst from her hair, and her scream echoed through an ethereal nightmare.

Zepallo appeared as a dark cloud floating in the sky, "If you think this vision of your mother's horror is terrifying, just wait until you try to move against me. A speech to the United Nations? There is nothing you can say that will alter the course of this campaign. You're a boy, a gifted and talented boy, but a boy nonetheless! I think you might want to think twice before you open your mouth. Your mother's life depends on it!"

With that, the dark cloud dissipated and the vision of Sara exploded in a shower of iridescent sparks. The streaming colors and the smooth hum returned. The other *seers* wrapped their arms around Adrian and guided him towards their destination. They could feel him sobbing.

As they approached the Island of Manhattan, Master Chi slowed their movement and the other *seers* surrounded Adrian, each facing their friend. Tears rolled down his cheeks, his chest heaved as he wept, and he could not look into their eyes.

Master Chi reached out and gently placed his hand on Adrian's shoulder and touched his chin with a crooked finger. "Look into my eyes and concentrate!"

Suddenly, he saw a vision of the thorny bush with the wonderful berries. He was gasping for air but his eyes snapped into focus. "Mother?"

"It was only a vision created by Zepallo and his dark technology. It wasn't real!"

Adrian looked around the circle. Simian, Mary, and Alius helped him to invade the lair beneath Central Park to rescue Raffe. The others joined together to return his own spirit to his body and defeat the Dark Forces on Morgan's Knot. They had triumphed against the Dark Lord and they would do so again.

The young *seer* sighed, "We will do what we must and we'll do it together."

The other *seers* wrapped Adrian in a hug and moved off to the General Assembly of the United Nations.

~

Lord Robbins pushed up the sleeve of his jacket and checked the time on his heavy gold watch, 2:59 PM. A sense of mild panic raised a sheen of perspiration on his brow. Arranging this time, for a speech by a young boy, had cost him political capital and, if Adrian didn't show up, he would surely be the laughingstock of the Assembly.

The Ambassador gazed around the room and there was not an empty seat in the house. Rumors spread throughout the day that the young man, who introduced them to the Balance and the world of the animals, was coming to speak again.

Now, animals represented all of the inhabited continents, including penguins from Antarctica, and the Council accepted their opinions and advice as they would any of the other diplomats. The world had taken one step towards a better life for every living thing but it was only a beginning.

Lord Robbins arranged for Suzanne and her son to fly in from Toronto and she informed her friends from the underground, who were all sitting in seats just behind the Canadian Ambassador's desk. They had never shared the secret of the other events that occurred the day that Adrian first spoke before this assembly. Suzanne reached out the touched Lord Robbins on the shoulder, "If Adrian said that he would be here, he will."

The Ambassador smiled nervously and looked at his watch again, 3:00PM. Suddenly, a hush rolled across the chamber, as everyone looked up to follow eight bodies flitting above their heads in what appeared to be a slow, gentle aerial ballet. They flew a lazy figure eight near the ceiling and swooped low, their robes almost brushing those seated on the floor, before spiraling together behind the podium.

Adrian allowed himself to descend very slowly until he was standing behind the microphone, which was pointed above his head. He could hardly see over the dais and looked to the side of the platform, where a technician was standing. He held up his hand to indicate that he wanted a hand microphone. The man brought one to him and turned it on. "Thank you," said Adrian.

"Ladies and Gentlemen, and, my friends, the Ambassadors for the Animal World, I come to speak with you today about the state of our world. Perhaps it's better that I'm a child, because I have no reason to speak anything but the truth."

There was warm applause.

"We live in a world of fear. Everyone is afraid of not being enough, or not having enough, or that someone will come and take what they do have. We fear our governments, who are supposed to represent and protect us. We fear the teachings and the leaders of our religions, yet we obey their dictates. We fear our neighbors and lock our doors to keep them out. Turn on your television or open a newspaper and you'll find endless stories about all the things that we should be afraid of…terrorists, wars, famine, crime, racial violence, economic warfare that results in jobs being lost, security being erased, and a future without hope. Our whole world is built on fear."

There was silence in the room.

"I come from a place where everyone cares for everyone else, where there are no locks on the doors because your neighbors are as close as family. It's a place where man and nature work together and everyone benefits from that cooperation, a place of boundless energy and bountiful harvests, where people work hard for their mutual benefit, and there are some with rather unusual abilities," Adrian smiled as he turned to gesture to his friends, who were still hovering behind the podium.

"I'm sure that the representatives in this room know far more about the current state of affairs in the world than I do...but we've all watched the news and seen the confrontation between the Third World countries and the Industrialized Nations. There can be no doubt their grievances and desperation are real and true, because the world has been divided into those who have and those who have not. There is no representation by and for the people...your people, my people, or their people. Our countries are governed not by our elected officials but by giant corporations, whose only interest is the size of the profits they produce for their shareholders."

The room burst into applause with a few whistles and cheers.

"Which brings me to another thing that our leaders have avoided and it's time to change. Our world isn't capable of endlessly supplying us with the raw materials that we consume and then discard which pollutes the air and the water. It's time for mankind to start repaying the generosity of our planet. We know how to produce energy without poisoning the environment. We know how to grow food without putting chemicals in the soil. We know how to produce reliable and reusable goods without creating mountains of trash. We know how to do this the right way and there's no reason that we should continue to do things the old way. Why shouldn't everyone share in the bounty and the responsibility for our world?"

The room exploded with thunderous applause, especially from the nations represented by the New Coalition.

"It's been reported, recently, that all of the military budgets of all of the countries in the world amount to trillions of dollars a year! What could we do to improve the quality of life for everyone on the planet with an extra trillion dollars or two? It's time to stop investing in guns and bombs and new ways to exterminate each other and begin putting that money into programs that will provide a better life for everyone.

There are many here who would rather that I didn't say that it's time for the people…all of the people…to take back the responsibility for themselves, their families, their neighbors, their communities, and their nations. Even in the Industrialized Nations, the turnout for their elections is embarrassing at best. If the citizens don't like what's going on, show up and vote!

If you look at a picture of the world from space, you realize that there are no lines marking where one nation begins and another ends. We are one world. We are one nation. We are one people!

These friends behind me represent small societies from every corner of the planet and, in each of their homes, there is peace, there's harmony, there's cooperation for the common good, and the animals are an integral part of that balance. It could be this way everywhere…it should be this way everywhere.

I wouldn't presume to tell anyone what they should believe or what path they should follow, but I will say that it's time for all of the people to live, as they know they should live, not as they've been forced to exist! There's plenty of everything for everyone, if we're willing to join together, to work together…to be one people…to be one nation…to be one world."

The audience was standing, clapping furiously, and there were smiles on the faces of the ambassadors representing both sides of the current conflict.

"Not too long ago, I stood here and told you about the world of the animals. At first, many of you were frightened by the creatures who invaded this chamber but now, the natural world has their own representatives and no one seems frightened anymore."

The animals laughed and the ambassadors nodded their agreement.

Adrian raised his hand for quiet, "The last time that I spoke to you, I confronted Palloze, the spokesman for the New Coalition. You witnessed his aggression towards us and saw a glimpse of his true colors. I say to you that he does not represent your best interests. He has only one client and that's himself. His goal is to rule the world and, if he's allowed to continue, he will succeed."

There were murmurs in the audience, whispers behind cupped hands, and eyes that glanced away, as Adrian scanned the representatives of the New Coalition countries.

"I'm a young boy and what do I know of these things? I'm a young boy who has battled this man and all that he stands for...I have suffered his cruelty and I recognize the person that he is in his soul. If you allow him to continue, you'll know the evil that he represents and you'll bear the consequences. He would gladly see the two sides go to war over the current confrontations. He wins either way and all of you will lose."

The crowd reacted with rumblings and muted shouts.

Adrian let the commotion roll through the enormous room for a moment, "You know, I honestly don't think that adults get it. I don't think they can conceive of a person so dark or a force capable of complete annihilation nor do I think they can comprehend the concept of a world at peace."

"I'll tell you who does understand, the children and the animals! So I call on the children, each and every one of them, it's time to make your parents understand. It's time for you to take them by the hand to show them the power of the individual and what the future might hold for everyone. Those of you in the countries where there are demonstrations and riots against foreign forces and bases within your country...go to these places and stand between the foreigners and the crazy adults. Make them stop their protests and escort those forces to safety. Those soldiers aren't in your countries because they choose to be.

They're there because they've been brainwashed by their governments to believe that it is their duty.

The adults only follow those who they believe have wealth and power. The children know how to lead because they're honest and because they haven't been infected with the lies that the adults have transformed into convenient truths. The animals know how to work together without destroying the wonders around them. Together the animals and the children could show the grownups how to create a better world, how to live a better life."

Adrian looked up to see the vision of his mother, squirming snakes slithering over her body, the purple flames shooting from her scalp, the look of terror in her eyes. It glowed in the shadows at the back of the room. He turned to glance at Master Chi, who was floating behind his right shoulder. The other *seers* were holding hands and staring intently at the image. The Master nodded his head, he could see it too.

Adrian pointed at the shimmering nightmare, "Can anyone else see the image that I'm seeing?"

Everyone in the audience turned to stare at the cloud that hovered in midair. Lord Robbins turned to look back at Adrian, his jaw slack with astonishment.

"This is an image that Palloze projected to me just before I arrived here to speak to you. He would rather that we didn't have this conversation and he'll go any lengths to stop me from revealing the truth. That's my mother, she was kidnapped yesterday by the man you know as Palloze. I know him as Zepallo, the Dark Lord of a vast army called Legio Obscurum."

There were murmurs and gasps from the audience.

"I'm frightened by what he might do to her. My heart wants to find a way to rescue her and to take my revenge. He doesn't want the world to know the truth about what he's doing. He doesn't want me to tell you about all the wonderful things that are truly possible, that the world can and should be a better place for every living creature. It can be a paradise for everyone, if we all work together, if we all stand together to say that we're finished with fear, finished with being manipulated by our governments and big business, who benefit from the inequities of our existence. We have no use for people like Palloze, who breed fear and destruction. We're free to make the world what it ought to be, together."

The people in the chamber were torn between Adrian's words and the image hovering at the rear of the room. There was scant applause and a quiet rumble rippled across the chamber.

Adrian turned to his friends and smiled, "It's not up to me to make these changes. It's up to you. There's nothing to fear when we all join together for the common good. The promise of tomorrow isn't about politics, or economics, or religion, or beliefs. It's about working together to repair our world and care for each other. I call on every child in every corner of the planet. Teach your parents. Show them what can and should be."

He looked down at Suzanne, who was holding her baby to her shoulder. The look in her eyes conveyed hope that could not mask her fear. She understood the message but she was horrified by the shimmering image of his mother.

Adrian's lips curled into a small smile, which could not conceal the pain in his eyes. He reached a hand to her and levitated her onto the stage. Turning back to the audience, which was murmuring in confusion, he said, "You've watched us fly through the air. You've glimpsed a small piece of the wonders of the Balance and you've seen hints of the horrors that will spread across the planet unless you, all of you, stand up for what is right and true. I say to you, there's a better way. It's within your reach and we're ready to help you to find the correct path but you have to take the first steps.

You must take the responsibility from those who claim to represent you, from those who tell you how to live and what to believe, and you must stop being afraid! The one thing that you should fear is what will happen if you do nothing! The world can be the paradise that God intended or we can destroy it and ourselves. The choice up to you."

The young *seer* did not hesitate. He winked at Jack and led Suzanne and her son behind the podium, where they joined hands with the other *seers*. A moment later, they were gone.

The room exploded in pandemonium. Everyone had an opinion about what just occurred, what they just witnessed, and what they believed had been said. Each had their own interpretation and wasted no time in expounding on it.

Jack walked up to Lord Robbins and tugged on his sleeve, "Sir."

The Canadian Ambassador turned and greeted Jack with a firm handshake and a friendly smile, "How are you?"

"We're doing well, thank you," replied Jack. His clothes were clean, if not new, and he appeared healthy and well fed. "If you'd like to have a word with young Adrian, I think that it can be arranged but we must hurry."

The Ambassador looked into his eyes, "I am at your service, Sir. With all of this commotion, I think we can sneak out of here without anyone noticing. They're all too busy arguing!"

"Please step this way," replied Jack, as he and his friends walked up the aisle, out through the lobby, and down the stairs to the subway. Once they reached the platform, they turned right, jumped down onto the track bed and along the rails for about one hundred yards, where they came to the unfinished section that provided access to the tunnels leading to the chamber with the Golden Crystal.

Anthony Robbins had never ventured into the bowels of New York before, let alone with a band of homeless people that he had only met once. He was out of shape and out of breath, when they finally settled into a slow march along a darkened channel. "Do all of you still live down here?"

"Yes, we do," replied an older woman. "We made a promise to protect the Powers and that's what we're doing."

Jack stopped and turned to the Ambassador, "Sir, before we reach our destination, I would ask that the things you're about to learn and the things you see remain our secret. It's really best for everyone...but you'll understand soon enough."

Robbins smiled, "I will honor your request, Jack. To tell you the truth, I have no reason not to...as you said, it's probably best for everyone."

"That it is, Sir," smiled Jack, turning back into the tunnel to lead the little group up ladders and down ramps until they came to the chamber.

They could hear voices from inside and found Adrian and the other *seers* standing around the giant Golden Crystal. Everyone was admiring the baby and Alius and Suzanne were huddled in quiet conversation.

Lord Robbins noticed the intense glow and a bristling breeze but hesitated for a moment, before he looked up into the radiance of the spinning *orb* and gasped, "What is this?"

"It's a Golden Crystal," replied Jack. "There are three others, of course, red, blue, and green. Oh, and there's still the Black one."

Adrian overheard the conversation and walked up to the Ambassador, "Welcome. I know that this isn't exactly the type of meeting room that you're accustomed to but perhaps it's appropriate for you to be introduced to the Crystal and to understand a little of what I tried to explain to the Assembly and to...our friend yesterday. Maybe you'll be able to explain it to him in terms that he might understand."

"I'm not quite sure whether I should be concerned or feel privileged to be here."

Adrian laughed, "A little of both, I think. The last time we were here, we destroyed Zepallo's...or Palloze's command center, which is powered by a giant Black Crystal. This, on the other hand, is a Golden Crystal. Black Crystals are negative and all the other Crystals are positive...in all senses of the word. Where we come from, the Crystals provide more power than we might ever need. It can be the same for everyone across the globe."

Robbins' eyes twinkled, "An unlimited, never-ending power source?"

"The problem is that the Dark Forces use the Black Crystals to provide the power necessary for their ambitions. If someone, Zepallo for instance, were to gain control of all of the Crystals, there would be no force on the planet that could compete. He would have absolute control."

The smile on the Ambassador's face dimmed, "You mean that this is what he's really after, control of all of the Crystals throughout the world?"

Everyone in room had grown quiet and attentive, as they joined the conversation. Alius nodded, "We've foiled him several times but I'm not sure we have the forces or the power to keep pushing them back. One failure and the game is up."

Master Chi said, "Mr. Ambassador, please understand that these Powers have been used since the beginning times. We could give you a history lesson that might take days, weeks, or even years. Perhaps the easiest way to allow you to understand is to provide some simple examples. On the positive side, you've heard the legend of Atlantis?"

"Yes."

"Well, Atlantis was very real. In fact, the books that we use to understand and harness the Powers of the Crystals have been handed down since the eruption ripped the Island of Atlantis apart. Most of us have studied those texts. They offer an understanding of the world as it should be."

"I don't believe it," murmured Robbins. "I do…but…"

"On the other side, an example might be the rise of Nazi Germany and the extermination of millions of innocent people. They used the Powers of the Black Crystals."

"Oh, my…"

"Used wisely, these energies can and will benefit all mankind. In the wrong hands, those same powers have been turned to create the darkest chapters in our history."

Adrian interrupted, "We hope to bring the wonders that we know to be true and real to all of the people of the world but, first, they have to accept the responsibility for themselves. Our good intentions run headlong into the reality that there are some people who will find a way to make a profit or use the powers to install themselves in positions of authority. We can't allow that to happen."

"I think I'm beginning to understand," sighed the Canadian Ambassador.

"It's far more complex than we have time to explain," injected Simian. "In simple terms, there's been a secret war going on for thousands of years, between the Light and the Dark. We represent one side and Zepallo and his comrades, the other. When you have time, consider the darkest moments in the history of man and you'll see the Power of the Black Crystals."

Mary added, "Not long ago, there was a terrific battle between the two sides. Adrian defeated Zepallo in a titanic struggle but that was only one battle. There will be more, unless the people of the world unite and stand together against the Dark Forces."

Lord Robbins appeared to be at a loss for words. He seemed to believe what he was hearing but, as with everyone who is introduced to the Powers, this new reality was overwhelming and it showed in his momentary loss of that diplomatic poise.

Adrian smiled, "I know how you feel. I only learned about these things a little over a year ago. Think of it this way, there are parallel worlds that have existed, in the same time and the same space, since the beginning of human existence. We've lived in one and you've lived in another. They're both real but our world has remained hidden from the rest of the population through the ages, because the citizens of the world were not ready to assume the responsibility that goes with these wonders. Now we've come to a moment in time, when they'll have to understand or all will be lost. We've defended the Power of the Light, secretly, and we'll continue to do so...but Zepallo has introduced another twist in this long struggle. Now, he's organizing major players in governments, financial institutions, and the major religions to become his surrogates, his army of Darkness. If there is a world war, he wins, no matter who loses."

Robbins looked around at the *seers* gathered in the chamber. From their expressions, he had to conclude that everything he was being told was true. There could be no doubt about their sincerity. "I think I comprehend what you are saying and the gravity of the current global situation. It's far deeper and more dangerous than any of us might have feared."

"There have been many times in history, when the Dark Forces came close to winning the war but each time they've been driven back at great cost. This is one of those moments, when the people of the world must make a decision that will affect everything from this instant forward," said Master Chi, softly. "We, as a species, must make a stand. Either we believe in the basic goodness of Man or we close our eyes and allow the Dark Lord to wrap the world in his shadow. It's a simple choice but, as you see, it's far more complicated than a young boy can explain in one speech. We have to find a way to make the people, the common people, of the world understand and, then, to act."

The Ambassador looked into Adrian's eyes, "I understand enough to offer my help. I'll talk to…our friend…personally, as soon as possible. I assume he knows how to reach you?"

Adrian laughed, "I'm not sure he does, actually. He doesn't seem to understand computers or the Internet very well. Perhaps you could assist him?"

Robbins laughed, "I'd be happy to lend a hand."

Adrian turned to Jack, "Would you be kind enough to show the Ambassador back to the United Nations?"

"I'd be honored!" laughed Jack.

Lord Robbins held out his hand, "I'd like to shake your hand and thank you for allowing me to understand a little of your world."

Adrian shook his hand, "It's not my world, it's our world. It belongs to everyone."

"I'll be in touch," replied Robbins, as he followed Jack out into the tunnels.

Adrian turned to Alius, "What have you learned about Suzanne's beautiful son, Tiffin?"

Alius smiled, "I don't know for sure but I think he has potential. I'd like them to meet the Professor."

The young *seer* smiled, "That could be arranged. In fact, everyone here has protected the Crystals, just as they promised. Although there's much that we must do, would you like to visit our home?"

Everyone replied, "Oh, yes, yes, we would."

He looked at his fellow *seers*. "There are eight of us. We could easily manage two each. What do you say?"

"Are you sure that you want to do this now?" inquired Raffe. "There are other battles to be fought."

"I know, but if we're going to teach the people of the world about our reality, then we have to start somewhere. Why not here...why not now?"

Simian looked at the eager faces of the small group and smiled, "We'll have you back before you know it!"

Jack returned, just as the group was forming a large circle. "What's happening?"

"We're going to visit Morgan's Knot!"

Chapter 13

Sara gazed around the giant dome at hundreds, perhaps thousands of purple workstations zipping through the space to hover, pulsing as if digesting information, before whizzing off to form another cluster. She had been confined in a clear bubble floating just outside the central podium, where Zepallo's technicians coordinated the efforts of the technicians. Data, news feeds, diagrams, images, and videos flickered and danced on giant screens that formed a radiant sphere inside the massive cavern a thousand feet below the surface.

Her host had been true to his word, she suffered neither abuse nor neglect. Anything she might need could be ordered by merely saying the words. Within moments, a worker on an aerial scooter would arrive to deliver whatever she ordered and she was transported to the women's bathroom upon request. A comfortable chair folded flat and the sphere could be frosted when she wanted to rest but she found herself mesmerized by the pictures and information flashing across the displays in mind-boggling arrays that washed the cave in a flickering blue cast.

Her attention was drawn to a large screen that displayed the world news, because the information on many of the other screens was incomprehensible, and, although her cell shielded all outside sound, she noticed the video news showed the United Nations building in New York and then the General Assembly room inside.

She was amazed to see eight familiar *seers* floating though the air and her son gliding gently to stand at the podium. He could not reach the microphone and motioned to the side. A technician appeared and handed him a microphone. He turned back to his audience and began to speak.

Frustrated, Sara shouted, "Audio!" hoping that her command would supply the sound. It did not. Instead, a female voice said politely, "How may I help you?"

"May I hear the audio of the International News that is being shown on your screen?"

"One moment, please."

Nothing happened.

The voice returned, "I'm sorry but my orders do not allow that information to be transmitted to your sphere. Please try again later."

Sara stared at the screen, transfixed with the image of her son moving about the platform and, from his expression, talking about serious things. She knew the earnest and convincing look from the many times he wanted to persuade her of something...usually something that he knew she would not approve.

The camera zoomed in on his face, as he pointed at the back of the room, and his eyes were filled with sadness and fear, emotions she rarely saw in her son. The perspective cut to a wispy vision. Sara gasped, realizing that she was watching a video of herself, with writhing snakes surrounding her body, strange purple flames shooting out of the top of her head, and her face contorted in terror.

"How could they have created an image of something that never happened?" She wondered. "Adrian must be frantic!"

Another camera panned across confused and anxious dignitaries, as they looked from the image to the dais and back again with fear and concern on many of their faces. Adrian appeared again, speaking calmly, although forcefully. Finally, he levitated a young woman, with a baby in her arms, onto the stage. They turned to the others, who were hovering in the air above the podium, and joined hands, disappearing into the vectors.

The camera swept over the crowd. The delegates seemed to be arguing and yelling at each other with passionate gestures and the expressions made her wonder whether the whole scene was going to evolve into an international brawl, like those that she had seen in the movies. Suddenly, the huge screen was filled with the practiced smile of the newscaster and Sara turned away, burying her face in her hands.

She felt relief that her son was safe, astonishment that he was speaking to a world forum when she knew he tended to be shy, and concern that he believed she was suffering the horrors in the video. She wondered whether she would ever get to hold him in her arms again but she was thankful he avoided the trap that Zepallo set for him.

~

Lord Robbins rose from his seat on the official Canadian Government jet and walked down the steps to a waiting limousine. The pavement was slick and a cold north wind buffeted the airport but the storm clouds were clearing and the moon was rising above the eastern horizon into a clear dark sky.

A special agent held the door, as the Ambassador slipped inside and found the imposing figure of his mentor waiting. The cowl of his dark robes hid everything but the intimidating glow of his blue eyes.

"We find that you have managed to place yourself in an interesting position," whispered Zepallo.

Robbins smiled, "It is rather odd to be invited to act as a liaison with the young *seer* by the President of the United States but the Powers work in mysterious ways."

"What did you learn from the boy?"

"He's on a mission to stop you, with the help of the entire population of the world. How did his speech come across on the television?"

"In some ways it was charming and convincing but, at the same time, he seemed like a boy telling his parents about some magical dream he had while he was sleeping. I don't think that it will have any effect on our plans but I'm more comfortable knowing you're standing between the young *seer* and the president."

"I was amazed to see the image that was projected at the rear of the Chamber. I assume that you had nothing to do with it.

"Believe what you like, although it is the same image that I conjured up for Adrian and his friends, as they approached New York. I want to maintain his state of panic. Having his mother as my guest will keep him off balance and prevent him from mounting a rescue mission on his own."

"Did you know that there's a group of street people guarding the Positive Crystals in New York?"

"Yes, they have no power and, to tell you the truth, they help to keep the curious out of those tunnels. We've sealed off our facilities and have an army of technicians working day and night to rebuild."

"I find that reassuring," said the Ambassador.

"What are you going to tell the president?"

"The truth. He undoubtedly saw the broadcast of young Adrian's speech and they did have a conversation yesterday, to which I was not invited. I'm sure that he'll want to maintain contact throughout this crisis and I'll be only too willing to provide whatever assistance he might require."

Zepallo sneered, "You will maintain contact with me! Meet me at the Memorial, when you've finished with Bartlett."

"As you wish."

Zepallo touched his fingertips to his brow and disappeared. The limousine sped through the city and the Ambassador watched the reflections of the lights of the monuments glittering across the pavement as he pondered the curious position that circumstances had presented.

He smiled to himself, "I'm standing in the eye of a hurricane. I can't change the intensity of the storm but I can guide it and that might be enough."

Two uniformed policemen on motorcycles escorted the sleek black car through stoplights, past lines of waiting cars, stopping only when they reached the gates of the White House. Lord Robbins was expected.

~

The vectors seemed smooth and there was no interference on the journey back to Morgan's Knot. Adrian struggled to maintain his

148

outward calm but his mind was replaying the images that Zepallo projected. There had to be a way to rescue his Mother and he could hardly wait to talk with the Professor to see whether they found a trail.

He turned to Master Chi, "I hate to ask but who projected that image on the wall of the Assembly Room?"

"We did," replied Master Chi, simply.

"Why?"

"Because the delegates and the world need to understand the danger that Zepallo represents. Too many people view him as the savior who will restore their place in the world."

"We could have shown the film that Ponte made."

"You decided that this was not the right time for that and we agreed, but the delegates needed a little push and this was a more subtle, yet powerful, way to convey that message without making it appear that you were involved. I guess we might have consulted you beforehand but there was no time and we all felt that it was the best contribution we could make to your speech. Incidentally, you did very well. I think a lot of people will understand."

"Thank you," said Adrian with a sheepish smile. "I was nervous."

"It didn't show and you chose your words wisely. Did your training help?"

The young *seer* smiled, "Yes, it did."

"Good. Orana would be proud of you."

They landed on the path outside the observatory just as the sun was setting in the west. The door swung open with a bang, as Ponte emerged, backlit by the glow of the lamps inside. "Well done! Well done! Welcome home!"

He looked around at the group accompanying the *seers*, "I see we have guests. Who are these people?"

Alius ran up the steps and put her arms around the old man's considerable girth, "These are the people who helped us during our last trip to New York. They've been protecting the Crystals in the tunnels and we've brought Suzanne and her baby, Tiffin. I want you to talk with her. He might be a candidate."

"Oh, lovely," replied the Professor as he hugged the little blond *seer.*

Adrian added, "We decided that it was time for the world to begin to learn about the Powers and what better group than these people, who have dedicated themselves to our cause, to have the inaugural tour!"

Ester appeared at the door, "Well, don't stand out there bring your friends in so we can get acquainted."

Adrian stepped through the door and turned to catch the expressions on the faces of their guests as everyone trooped into the parlor. He could feel their enchantment, as they gazed in wonder at the walls of books, the model of the solar system, the *orbs* lined up along one wall, and all the things that he found so intriguing every time he entered this room. The only thing that had changed since his first visit was the disappearance of the cages that held the birds and the snakes, replaced with two comfortable chairs on either side of a table that held the three-dimensional chess set.

The Professor turned to Ester, "M'dear, why don't you start the tour in the observatory, while I talk with the *seers* about what we've found?"

"I'd be happy to introduce them. Perhaps, I should start the lecture while we're up there?"

"Good idea," replied her husband.

The group from New York followed Ester through the dining room to the elevator and up to the observatory, while Ponte and Nanchez took the *seers* to the monitors.

"We noticed that your journey to the United Nations was intercepted. Did you have an encounter with our favorite villain?"

Sky replied, "Yes, he showed us that vision of Adrian's mother. It was certainly enough to frighten Adrian but he gathered himself and delivered a strong speech. We projected the image on the rear wall of the Assembly Chamber and hope it had the intended effect."

"It was frightening," replied Ponte.

"We've found some interesting things since you left, although we're not sure that they'll be of any real help," said Nanchez. Sammy was already powering up the *messengers*.

"On the first monitor, we have a trace of the trail that Zepallo left, when he kidnapped your mother. The vectors he followed seem to lead to a remote mountain in North Korea."

Adrian did not reply, as he watched the tracings projected in front of the *orb*.

Nanchez continued, "That's not exactly an accessible target. Not only is it protected by the Dark Forces but also by the Army of North Korea. That land is rugged and desolate for a hundred miles in every direction."

Ponte continued, "We've been watching their communications traffic and we might guess that they're using this new site as their command center."

"No one said that it would be easy," replied Adrian.

"We'll find a way," whispered Alius.

"There's more," said Nanchez. "It seems they might be rebuilding the lair in New York. We've noticed a lot of movement in the vectors around the site you destroyed."

"That doesn't surprise me either. I'm sure they're rebuilding the other one under the Caucasus Mountains too."

Ponte continued, "Now that we know that Zepallo did, indeed, intercept you, these tracings show that he followed you to New York and, after the speech, continued on the Washington, D.C."

Adrian was stunned, "I wonder who he was meeting?"

"Answer that question and you'll have an insight into his influence within the government of the United States."

Alius turned to Adrian, "I think we can rule out the president. He seemed to be genuinely astonished at some of the things we told him but it wouldn't surprise me to find that Zepallo's contact is someone close to President Bartlett."

"I agree," replied Adrian. "The question is...who?"

Simian had been quiet, listening to the conversation, "The 'who' might be many. The tentacles of the Dark Forces reach into every sphere of influence."

"I agree," said Master Chi, "but this evidence suggests there's someone who can manipulate opinions at a very high level. If we could find this one, perhaps we could find a trail to others."

"Good point," replied the Professor, as he moved to the next monitor. "We also taped the speech and the commotion that occurred after you left." The video showed the group of *seers*, as they disappeared, and then panned across the room. Delegates were shouting and arguing their own interpretations of what had just occurred. A herd of animals could be seen leaving en masse in the background.

Adrian looked worried, "Maybe my speech wasn't such a good idea."

"My boy, you did your best and that's all anyone could ask. What your audience does with the ideas and information you provided is up to them," said the Professor in a reassuring tone. "Besides, these people are paid to argue and to protect the status quo. If the citizens of their countries understood the message, each of them will be out of a job. There hasn't been enough time for the news organizations to record the reaction across the world. We'll know more tomorrow."

"I've learned many things since I arrived on this island but patience is one I still have to work on," said Adrian quietly.

Nanchez wrapped a huge arm around the young *seer*, "M'boy, you've done some amazing things, since you began this journey, and you've matured way beyond your years. You turned my people from the Dark Powers, rescued your parents and the folks on the Island of the Children, connected all the nodes, gathered all these *seers* into a formidable force, helped destroy three...count 'em, three of the Dark Forces hidey-holes, and defeated the Dark Lord himself in hand-to-hand combat. I'd say you've come a long way in the past year but it's, obviously, not over yet."

The large man smiled down at Adrian, "Be proud of what you've done, what you've learned, and what you've become."

Adrian blushed, "Thank you."

"It is we who should thank you," said Alius.

The young *seer* was quiet, as he turned in a circle and looked into the eyes of his friends, and suddenly realized that what he needed most was the reassurance of his family. "I need to see my father, if that's alright with you. I'll be back in the morning. Take care of our guests and make my apologies."

He turned and walked out through the front door into the night. Calming himself, he rose into the air and slowly drifted south over the island to the House of the Four Seasons. He was reminded of those times, before he started to master his own powers, when he watched Magnus riding the thermals in lazy circles across the sky.

A cold salt-stained breeze wafted up the cliffs from the ocean and the island seemed calm and quiet. In the distance, he could see the lights, erected over the construction site, skittering across the waves. Somehow, he missed the groundbreaking for the next step in the progression of life on Morgan's Knot. He also missed most of the year at school and had no idea of when he might have the chance to go back to being a normal boy for a while. The idea of struggling to keep up with the expectations of his teachers, somehow, had very little meaning at the moment.

The world sat on the brink of disaster, his mother was being held hostage by his enemy, he had survived giving a speech before a worldwide audience, and he could not remember one word or phrase that he said. He could see the audience staring at him, the delegation of animals nodding their approval, the image of his mother writhing in agony shimmering in the shadows at the back of the room, and the intensity in the eyes of the other *seers*, as they merged their powers to project that vision to the whole world.

He thought back to his time under Orana's instruction and the lessons that might offer solutions to the challenges he faced. *"Somewhere in all of that, there's an answer and I must find it."*

He needed time to be alone, to be with his family, and to be sad that there wasn't more he could do, in this moment, to save his mother. He opened his senses and felt ripples of energy flowing across the globe, the quick vibration of new life and the slow deliberate rhythms of the aging. Deep pulses of anger thundered behind the jagged noise of uncertainty...and there seemed to be more insecurity than any other impulse. Grand movements were underway and no one had the power to guide the tide of humanity that would determine the future of civilization. Each of the billions of citizens would have to decide for themselves.

Adrian laughed to himself. In one way, the idea of the people deciding the future was terrifying and, yet, it might be the most democratic moment in the history of the planet. If nothing else, the future would be decided by each person, one at a time. They would join with other people, who had chosen the same course of action, and eventually, by the weight of sheer numbers, the leaders of the world would be forced to bow to the will of the masses...or they would do nothing and Zepallo would conquer the world without revealing Legio Obscurum.

Chapter 14

The president's personal secretary announced Lord Robbins and opened the door for him to enter the Oval Office. President Bartlett stepped from behind his desk to shake the Ambassador's hand, "Thank you for coming. I certainly appreciate your help."

"It has been my pleasure," smiled Robbins. "What did you think of the speech?"

"For a young man of his age, I think he handled it fairly well. It was honest and unscripted. The image of his mother was very powerful and frightening but his message was clear. For the first time in the history of the world, the responsibility for our future has been placed squarely on the shoulders of the common man...every common man."

"I agree, although each of us might be searching for new employment," laughed the Ambassador.

"You might be right but, to tell you the truth, I can't argue with the things he had to say. He touched on inequities that we, all of the industrial nations, should have dealt with long ago."

"Right you are."

"Did you have any other thoughts?"

"I'm afraid that my initial reaction was that some of what he said made him come across as a naïve boy but I honestly have no idea of what the reaction will be across the globe. Certainly, there's a part of me that wanted to root for him, especially when the image appeared at the back of the chamber, but my professional reaction was that the citizens of the world will never unite behind the message of a child. I know that I could be wrong but we should be prepared for the possibility that there is no reaction."

"You do have a point. What else?"

"Well, after the speech, one of the young homeless men and his friends, guided me through the subway tunnels to meet with Adrian. They were gathered in an abandoned chamber off one of the underground channels around a huge golden crystal spinning madly and balanced in mid-air a foot above the floor."

"He and his friend, Alius, told me about the Crystals and I found it hard to believe. I've consulted with a few of our top scientists and they scoffed at the idea of vectors and crystalline power sources. Maybe that's why we haven't made more progress to solve the problems that he spoke about."

"I tend to agree," continued Robbins. "They told me about the Powers and Zepallo's ambitions to control all of the Crystals."

"We might assume that the New Coalition is a front for that effort."

"If we are to believe young Adrian, then, yes, that seems to be the case. I haven't had time to contact our public relations people. What's the reaction to the speech?"

"My people are monitoring the response but they admit there isn't enough to work with yet. My speechwriters want me to make a response but Adrian wasn't speaking to me...he was speaking to everyone else," said the president with a wave of his hand. "All we can do is wait."

"The hardest part of our jobs."

"You're right about that. The gears of government work slowly, mechanically, and there's no way that even the most powerful leaders in the world can make it move any faster."

"Whatever happens, the world is about the change. The center of power is shifting."

The president stared at his guest, "What was your impression of our young friend?"

Lord Robbins hesitated for a moment, "I find him mature beyond his years, knowledgeable in things that neither of us understand, possessing powers...like his ability to fly...that escape normal people, and...and, yet, he is still a boy in every sense of the word. I have to admit I find it rather terrifying that, in some ways, he holds the future of the world in his very young and inexperienced hands."

"Given the choice…between Adrian and Palloze, I think we must choose our young friend."

"We really don't know much about Palloze. My people have found very little history to follow. Adrian talked about mysterious Dark Forces and battles that have gone on for hundreds of years. There were some parts of his story that I found… incredible."

"Do you believe him?"

"I'm not sure that I believe everything he told me but I have nothing to which I might reference my reaction. Dark Forces, magical Crystals, wars that appear nowhere in written history, parallel worlds, and a mysterious cadre of good and evil wizards from all over the globe. It's the stuff of a great children's tale."

The president laughed, "I see your point, although I have to say that I don't agree. The things he talked about are the stuff of fiction but there is an honesty about him that makes you want to believe his story."

"Perhaps one day, we'll both know the truth about all of this."

"I think that day is coming sooner than either of us might hope."

"Tomorrow will be an interesting day, a day when great leaders will be forced to make hard choices, and those decisions will affect every man, woman, and child on the planet. Whether you follow the advice of children or find a more compelling way to deal with the torrent that's circling the globe, I don't envy you that responsibility but I know that you'll use your best judgment."

Bartlett smiled, "I thank you for setting up the speech and for coming to talk with me. I know you must be tired."

The Ambassador rose from his chair and extended his hand to the president, "I hope that we both of have a job when the sun comes up."

"We'll talk again tomorrow," replied the president, as he walked his guest to the door and showed him out.

Back at his desk, he hesitated until he knew his visitor had left the anteroom, and pushed the call button, "Natalie, could you come in for a moment?"

The door opened and his secretary walked over to his desk, "Yes, Mr. President?"

"Get the Director on the phone."

"Yes, Mr. President." She turned, walked through the door and closed it behind her.

Less than a minute later, there was a buzz. "I have Director Sloan on the line."

"Thank you," said the president, as he picked up the receiver. "Don, how are you?"

"I'm fine, Mr. President. How can I help you?"

"Ambassador Robbins is just leaving the White House. I'd like you to find out where he goes and who he sees in the next few hours."

"That is highly unusual, Mr. President."

"I know and I would hope, first, that my gut reaction is mistaken and, second, that your people can do this without being detected. That would certainly cause a stir in Ottawa."

"I'll see to it, Mr. President, and I'll get back to you."

"Thank you, Don. I appreciate your sensitivity in this matter."

Bartlett replaced the phone in its cradle and leaned back in his chair. Something did not seem right about his conversation with the Ambassador but he could not put his finger on it.

His reaction to the young *seer* had been, at first, tentative, but the more he heard from the young man, the more he believed in his honesty. His pretty young friend, Alius, had reinforced and clarified facts and references. It was obvious that they had not rehearsed their lines or their interaction and, at least from their point of view, all of it was true.

Idealism is the intoxicant of youth and reminiscence an elixir for the aging. He wondered about the Powers of the Crystals and how it might be possible for the greatest minds in the history of science to have missed a technology that has existed since the beginning of time. If the young people were telling the truth, the concept of the Garden of Eden was possible for all of God's children.

~

Adrian landed in the garden and gazed around at his home. The old farmhouse glowed in the moonlight glistening across the ocean from the horizon. The pale light shimmered on the surface of the water, a blustery wind rustled the grasses and the trees, and everything seemed calm and peaceful. There was an emptiness, a hole in the fabric of his life, and he knew that the feeling would continue until he found a way to rescue his mother. The rest of the world would have to wait.

He trudged up the steps into the kitchen, where he found the whole family, as well as Josh, Ian, Morgan, and little Kelly. Everyone smiled and clapped, as he walked through the door. Elsie jumped up and wrapped her arms around her nephew, "Well done, my boy, well done!"

Adrian blushed and hugged his aunt, "I just told them about the things that I've learned from all of you."

His father walked over and hugged him, "I am so very proud of you and I know that your mother would be too."

"Thank you."

Molly, Megan, and the other children hugged him and patted him on the back. He was thankful for their support but he would have given anything to hear these encouragements from his mother.

The twins grabbed a plate of chocolate-chip cookies, two bottles of juice and some glasses and led the way outside. All of the children huddled close together on the split-log benches, each with their own reaction to what Adrian told the world.

Josh said, "I hope they get the message but I'll bet they won't!"

"Oh, they'll understand," replied Megan. "They have to!"

Morgan wrapped an arm around Adrian's shoulders, "I'm just proud that you had the courage to stand up and say the things that needed to be said. Most adults wouldn't have had the nerve to do what you did."

"I just told the truth," said Adrian, modestly.

"You're becoming famous!" laughed Ian.

"You said it so well," added Molly. "You were...not emotional but passionate, righteous, and articulate!"

"I just liked seeing you on the *orb*," smiled Kelly.

Adrian reached over and patted her on the back, "Thank you, Kelly."

She leaned over to Adrian, "I sure am sorry about your mother."

"Thanks, I just wish I could figure out how to get her back."

"What if you didn't have to get her back?"

"What do you mean?"

Kelly stood up and took Adrian's hand, "Can I talk to you for a minute...alone?"

Adrian smiled, "Sure."

They walked around to the path near the vegetable garden, where they couldn't be seen. Kelly looked up at the young *seer*, "I think I know how we can get her back."

"I'm open to suggestions."

Kelly held up the golden watch that Dr. Stevens had given her, when they rescued Ester from the mountain, "This is a turnabout."

"What's a turnabout?"

"It allows the person wearing this watch to move around through time. Dr. Stevens has been teaching me how to use it. We could use it to go back to the time before your mother was kidnapped. We could change the things that happened."

"You mean we could go back and intercept her before Zepallo got her?"

"Yes."

"Are you sure that this is really possible?"

"I'm sure. I've been forward and backward in time. I've seen myself as a baby and I've seen you graduate from school. Your mother was there to see it too."

Adrian's lips curled into a tentative grin. "Tell me how this works."

"I can turn the watch backwards or forwards, depending on where in time I want to be. The only danger is that we can't allow ourselves to cross our own paths and we have to return to this exact moment, or we'll get lost in time."

"So you're telling me that you could turn your watch back to a time before the kidnapping and we could be there, waiting for Zepallo?"

"Yes," smiled Kelly.

"Is there anything else that I should know?"

"Well, the watch doesn't work like a normal clock. We'll only have a short period to do what we must and if we don't make it back to our starting point within the given time, I'm pretty sure we'll just disappear!"

"Oh…so, basically, you're telling me that if we get this wrong, we'll just vanish, like a puff of smoke?" inquired the young *seer*, with an inquisitive tilt of his head.

"Yup."

"Are you sure you know what you're doing?"

"I've watched the things that you've done for everyone on this island, for everyone in the world…even if they don't know it. I know I can get you there and I can get you back. The rest is up to you."

"Do I trust you with my life? I most certainly do! Let's go!"

"You can fly. I can control time. What time do you think your mother was taken?"

"I'd guess about six-thirty last night. We got back from our meeting about quarter to seven and she was already gone."

"Then let's try for six-fifteen," said Kelly, as she opened the pocket watch. "Hold on to me."

Adrian whisked his little friend across the fields of the island, as she turned the hands of the little clock backwards until they read six-fifteen the previous night. She looked up at Adrian, smiled, and pressed the winding stem. Everything around them moved like a high-speed movie in reverse. The moon sank into the horizon and the sun rose from the west and moved across the sky to the east. When the movement stopped, it was dusk.

As they soared across the plain to the village, the trolley stopped in a cloud of dust on the path. A dark figure approached the side of the wagon through the glow of the *orbs* and yanked his mother out onto the ground.

Adrian landed in the fog swirling in the light of the *orbs*, pushed Kelly into the tall grass, and levitated to the struggling adults. The saber, that Dadeus repaired, was in his pocket, the blaster ring on his finger.

Zepallo spun around to face the young *seer*, "So we meet again!"

"Let her go, this is between you and me."

Zepallo held Sara close and withdrew a long black crystalline saber from a sheath on his belt. He extended the blade to the tip to the young *seer's* nose, "Does this mean that you have chosen to die?"

Adrian stared at the glow of the black crystal sword and then at his adversary. Slowly, he lowered his hand, reached into the pocket of his robes, and wrapped his fingers around the handle of his sword.

The Dark Lord smiled, "It seems to me that you have several options here. First, you could join with your mother and me to take control of the world. Nothing could stop us and the rewards would be unending!"

Adrian could see the look of terror in his mother's eyes, as Zepallo continued, "The second possibility is that you could try to kill me but we both know that you don't really want to kill your mother. Firing a blast at me would be foolish."

He laughed a most horrible laugh, "The third is that you can choose to die. It's up to you!"

"You know I would never join you and we both know I defeated you the last time we met," He turned, pointing above the ridge, "You have power and experience. I have youth, energy, speed, creativity, and my belief in the power of the Light. Are you willing to risk a duel?"

In one fluid movement, he flipped upside down in the air, withdrawing his sword, and extending his blade to deflect Zepallo's, "I guess we'll have another chance to settle this!"

Sara bit Zepallo's wrist and struggled free, as the Dark Lord fired a blast at the young *seer*, singeing his newly mended robes. Zepallo grabbed after Adrian's mother, who was crawling across the ground, and rose into the air to face his young foe. Kelly ran out of the shadows, gathered Sara, and climbed into the trolley. A moment later, they were rolling down the path towards the House of the Four Seasons.

Zepallo thrust forward, in classic form, and Adrian spun around the outstretched blade in a corkscrew. Sparks flew in showers, as the two blades clashed, Zepallo exploiting his size and strength, Adrian his speed and quickness.

The trolley had only traveled a hundred yards when Sara slammed on the brakes and jumped out, as the two *seers* flew higher and higher, tumbling through the darkness, silhouetted in front of the moon. Kelly slid off the seat and ran to wrap her arms around Sara's waist, "It's the Darkness and the Light."

Adrian's mother could not respond but knelt down to hug Kelly and stare with awe and terror at the battle in the sky.

The crystal swords clashed, spewing brilliant embers across the fields, as the two warriors vied for position in a tangle of bodies flailing through the air. Silhouetted in the moonlight, only their size and the color of their blades identified one from the other.

Sara squeezed Kelly and gasped each time Zepallo advanced, forcing Adrian backwards across the night sky. The Dark Lord had the advantage of his maturity, strength, and experience, but her son was quicker, spinning and soaring to deflect powerful lunges of the black crystal sword and jets of purple charges.

After a brutal clash, Zepallo backed away and fired a single blast. Adrian screamed and doubled over in the pain, as the round grazed the side of his chest beneath his arm. Grimacing, the young *seer* folded his body into a ball and began spiraling wildly through the air, as the Dark

Master rushed in for the kill. He fired another blast but his target was moving too fast and the streaming charge missed its mark.

Dazed by the wound, Adrian knew that he had to regain control, if he was going to survive. He heard Master Chi's advice, "If you truly believe in the Power of the Light…if you truly believe in yourself, you will never be defeated."

A vision of the scars on the body of that three-hundred-year-old man appeared and he knew this would not be his final battle. He struggled through the pain, spiraled through the air, and focused on the Dark Lord's face. The essence of the confidence, he felt before and during their last confrontation, flooded through his body. The evil smile melted and a moment of indecision flashed in those blue eyes, as Zepallo aimed and hesitated. The Master was distracted from the moment, confused by the young *seer's* movements. Adrian heard Magnus' instructions, "You have to be strong of heart, fearless, and proud!" and flew directly for his enemy at top speed. Oblivious to the wind whistling past his ears and whipping through his hair, he focused on the cold hard eyes glowing in the twilight. The blades of their swords clashed in an explosion of energy, as the young *seer* soared past, and the Dark Lord spun to his right.

Stretching out his arms and legs, Adrian slowed his rotation, took a deep breath, and fired a single blast that ripped through the darkness…a flaming ball of energy scorching the air as it flew. He grimaced and clamped his arm against the wound on his side, suspended in the air, unable to take his eyes off the trace. A look of terror flashed through Zepallo's eyes, as the charge closed on its target and tore through his right hand.

The sound of his roar rumbled across the plain with the growl of a mighty grumble of thunder. His black sword glittered, in the last rays of sunset fading behind the ridge, and tumbled through the air, clattering into the ditch. Zepallo's eyes twitched in shock and agony, as he gazed up at his adversary in disbelief, before disintegrating in a shower of gray sparks cascading over the trolley and sizzling across the gravel.

A moment later, Adrian crashed on the path and crumpled to the ground. Sara and Kelly rushed to him. His robes glistened with blood from the wound on his chest and he struggled to sit. Sara wrapped her arms around her son and tried to lift him into the trolley.

Kelly looked down at her watch, "We don't have time for the trolley. We have to be back at the House of the Four Seasons in three minutes."

She knelt down in front of Adrian, "Pay attention! You have to get us back there before our time runs out!"

The young *seer* tried to concentrate. Kelly's words echoed from far away, reverberating around the inside his skull. Finally, he grasped what she was saying and attempted to stand. He felt dizzy and his vision blurred, as he leaned on his mother, "Time's all screwed up but we have to get back to the House of the Four Seasons right now."

"I don't understand," protested Sara. "You're not fit to go anywhere!"

"We have no choice. There isn't time to explain but we can make it, if we hurry," said Kelly. "But don't...please don't, under any circumstances, tell anyone how we did this. You have to promise!"

"Of course, but what about the trolley?"

"It's already there," said Adrian, wrapping his good arm around Kelly, who held on to Sara. They lifted into the air, flitting from side to side like a bird with a damaged wing flying into a gale but drifting slowly towards the old farmhouse. The little girl opened her watch, "Come on Adrian, we have to hurry. You can go faster than this!"

The young *seer* was weak and woozy from the loss of blood gushing from his lesion but he focused on the lights in the farmhouse and willed himself along the beacon. They crashed near the vegetable garden and Adrian rolled on his back, groaning.

Kelly looked at the pocket watch again, "Twelve seconds to spare. I knew you could do it!" She turned, as the two of them levitated out across the plain, put a hand over his mouth, and looked up at Sara. "Shhhh...we can't let them see us."

"But...they're you?"

She hooked a thumb over her shoulder, "That was us going to save you about an hour ago. We're back to real time now but we arrived just a few seconds early."

Kelly and Sara struggled to help him up, first to one knee, then on both feet. They stumbled around the side of the old farmhouse to find his friends exactly where they left them.

Morgan jumped to her feet and ran to her friends, "We wondered where you'd gone but what happened to you?"

"It's a short story," joked Adrian, collapsing to his knees.

Molly and Megan stared at their aunt, "but you were...kidnapped."

Without missing a beat, she said, "We don't have time for that right now, someone run and call Dr. Stevens. We'll be needing his help."

They carried Adrian across the yard to the kitchen door, which flew open and John ran down the steps. He wasn't sure whether to hug his wife or help her carry their son into the house. "You're safe," he whispered, with a kiss on her cheek, taking Adrian in his arms. The whole family followed, as he carried his son upstairs.

The bedroom door swung open with a concerned, "Oh my, what's happened to Master Adrian?"

John placed him on the bed and lifted his arm to inspect the wound.

Elsie hugged her sister, "I don't know what's just happened. Maybe I don't want to know...but I'm glad that you're back in this house, safe and sound."

Sara glanced across the room to little Kelly's impish grin and then to her sister, "I'm not sure that I know either but we'll have to sort that out later. Right now, I want to know that Adrian is all right. We've been through this too many times lately."

The two women pulled off Adrian's tattered robes and Elsie fetched a washcloth to clean the wound. The door announced Dr.

Stevens, who stared at Sara for a moment, then looked down at little Kelly, "Have you been up to mischief again?"

Kelly looked down, shuffling her feet, then smiled her biggest smile, as she touched the watch hanging by a golden chain from her neck and reached her hand into the pocket of her dress to reveal the handle of a mighty black sword, "Once in a while, the smallest person gets a chance to be the hero."

The doctor shook his head and patted her on the back, before turning to the bed to inspect his patient, "Adrian, we have to stop meeting like this. Now let me see what you've done to yourself this time."

He tut-tutted several times, as he reached into his bag and withdrew a sterile cloth and a bottle of his healing waters. "Let's see if this might help."

Chapter 15

Ambassador Robbins walked out of the White House and stepped into the waiting limousine. The black car turned into traffic as a taxi pulled in behind it. After two blocks, the taxi turned right but another moved in two cars behind the Ambassador's. Three blocks later, it was replaced by another.

Neither Lord Robbins nor his driver were aware that they were being followed. He instructed the young man in the black cap to pull in at the Lincoln Memorial.

The ambassador gathered his coat around his body against a cold gale and climbed the steps to the commanding statue. Hidden spotlights made it appear that Lincoln was staring across the pools in the Mall to the Washington monument. Robbins walked around to the left, as he reached the top step, and disappeared behind the figure. His mentor was standing on a stone that rose up out of the darkness, his hands were hidden in his robes and his voice was deep and raspy, "What have you learned?"

"The president seems to believe young Adrian, although he's the first to admit that there's little that he or any leader can do until the will of the people is heard. They may ignore the young man's speech or they may take it to heart. We'll just have to wait to see what happens tomorrow."

The Dark Lord held up the stump of his right hand, "This is what their young savior is capable of doing. Tomorrow may be too late, unless we can move our people to lead the protesters to riot!"

Lord Robbins stared at the bloody stump, "My Lord, you're wounded."

"You fool, he's taken his mother back. Somehow, he manipulated time and this is the result!"

"I'm afraid I don't understand. How could he manipulate time?"

The Master was exasperated, "Never mind. Get in touch with our people and see what you can do to force a confrontation on the front lines. If we can't control the masses, perhaps we can control what the media reports. A battle or many battles with lots of casualties should get things back on track. Local citizens will react, if they believe their brothers and sisters and children have been attacked by foreign soldiers."

"I'll do what I can," said Lord Robbins quietly.

At the far end of the monument, an older couple posed for photographs they were taking of each other. The old woman fussed and waved at her husband to move this way and then the other way until he was in just the right position to allow her to get a clear shot of the two men hiding in the shadows behind the statue.

The compact telephoto lens brought their faces into clear focus. The president would enjoy their snapshots before morning.

~

Dawn at the U.S. Military Facility: Desert Fox - 200 miles north of Riyadh, Saudi Arabia.

One by one, private cars gathered into a pack, speeding north on the desolate unbending road plowing straight into the desert. Small children peered out of the windows and waved to each other. Their frustrated parents sat in the front seats staring straight ahead. After twenty-four hours of constant heckling, they had given in to their children's incessant demands to be taken to the protests that were threatening to turn into full-scale riots.

The cars slowed and parked several hundred yards from the main gate. A large crowd was shouting and jostling to push past armed guards, who stood at the ready behind the barricade. The Americans could not back down but everyone could see that they were terrified by the angry mob.

The children piled out of the cars and marched through the crowd, followed by a hush that rolled through the throng of protesters, as the children made their way to the front. Their parents reached to restrain them but they were determined, and, holding hands, they formed a line between the soldiers inside the fence and the protesters outside.

A little girl with long black hair and huge dark eyes stepped to the front, "You all heard Adrian's speech, so why are you here? You know as well as we do that these people would rather be at home with their families. They didn't come here voluntarily, they came because they were ordered by their government. It's our duty to escort them to safety. You have a choice, you can help us to do what is right or you can kill us!"

The protesters lowered their signs, their clubs, and their fists. The children turned around to face the soldiers inside the gate.

"It's time for you to leave our country. Go in peace but go now!"

The guards lowered their guns and turned back into the base. In the distance, the crowd could hear the engines of several large aircraft taxiing to the runway.

Large groups of children appeared at the gates of the American base in Guantanamo, Cuba…on either side of the demilitarized zone between North and South Korea…in the Sudan between tribes who had been slaughtering each other for years…along the border between Pakistan and India, who had been fighting over Kashmir for decades…Beijing's Tiananmen Square was filled to overflowing and thousands crowded into Red Square in Moscow, each child bearing a single flower…they gathered around the presidential palace in Argentina, where angry mobs protested political corruption that had destroyed the economy, leaving the vast majority of the population without food, clean water, or electricity. Children surrounded Parliament and overflowed Downing Street in London, marched through the Champs Elysees in Paris, invaded Congress and crowded around the White House in Washington. They appeared, reverently, in those places held most holy by every religion. In most cases, huge herds of animals appeared in support of the children, surrounding and dispersing the crowds of adults. There were hundreds of confrontations that day but not one child was assaulted or injured.

For the first time in the history of the world, the children were not being ignored or banished into silence, their voices and opinions were being heard by the leaders of every nation, every tribe, and every religion. Their message was simple and straightforward, put an end to the inequalities that have pitted one nation against another for centuries, create a true world-wide democracy that represents the needs of the common people, return every nation's troops to their own soil in safety and in peace, and dedicate the incredible resources of the world to creating a better life for every living creature.

Confronted with the wisdom of the innocents and relentless reporting, the adults had no choice but to concede. Perhaps, someday, the history books might view this moment as the first step in Man's journey back to Eden.

The Cast of Characters

Adrian – son of John and Sara – long and lanky, with blond hair and intense blue eyes

John – Adrian's father – a large man with dark hair and dark eyes, sailor and ship designer

Sara – Adrian's mother – blond, blue eyes, housewife, grew up on Morgan's Knot, daughter of the former *seer,* Paul

George – Adrian's uncle – tall strong, rough hands, salt and pepper hair

Elsie – Adrian's aunt and Sara's sister

Molly and Megan – George & Elsie's twin daughters – blond curly hair blue eyes, a year younger than Adrian

Morgan Keelty – sister of Josh – tall, long curly brown hair, green eyes

Joshua Keelty – Morgan's brother – dark eyes, jet-black hair,

Ian Sheridan – Kelly's brother and Adrian's second cousin – tall, slender

Kelly Sheridan – Ian's younger sister – incredible smile, brown eyes, blond curls

Spot and Dusty – dolphins

Professor Ponte – Keeper of the Powers on Morgan's Knot, astronomer, teacher, and Adrian's mentor

Ester – Ponte's wife - highly intelligent and Ponte's equal

Tic – talking black and white tomcat, Adrian's guide in the animal world

Brandy – Keelty's Irish setter

Travis – harbormaster

Jasmine – Travis' fishing trawler

Dr. Stevens – doctor on the island

Mrs. Stevens – doctor's wife and seamstress constructing diving suits

Mrs. Green – seamstress constructing diving suits

Nancy Smith – seamstress constructing diving suits

Daphne & Dante – deer

Damien – their foal

Beggar – small bear

Magnus – golden eagle

Harriet & Harry – hawks

The Book of Wisdoms – The Golden Book on Morgan's Knot

The Book of Knowledge – The Silver Book used by the *Others* to master the Dark Powers

Jamaica

Simian – Jamaican *seer*, Sammy's uncle

Sammy – Simian's nephew – young Keeper in training

Lorraine – Simian's wife

The *Others*

Alius – daughter of Jofre – the *Other's seer* - petite, blond, blue eyes, tough, independent, and beautiful

Jofre – father of Alius and Master of the *Others* – a huge domineering man with white eyes

Mandor – Supervisor of Production and Security – dark eyes, long straight white hair

Nanchez – Keeper of the Dark Powers – a giant of a man with white hair, dark eyes

The Island of the Children

Raffe – young, athletic, and naïve *seer* from The Island of the Children

Gabrielle – leader of the Underworld – Mary's husband, long white hair and beard

Dadeus – Keeper of the Powers for the underworld

Mary – Gabrielle's wife, *seer*

Morag and Jim – Raffe's parents

Book of Natural Balance – The Golden Book on the Island of the Children

Additional Characters

Sky – tiny Thai *seer* – from the Temple of Spiritual Harmony, Thailand

Master Chi – M*aster seer* - Temple of Ancient Truths – Himalayas

Master Jung – slender old Keeper – Temple of Ancient Truths

Mantis – Sky's mentor

Shambala – African *seer*

Mambazi – little girl in Shambala's village

Lala & Maze – *seers* from the southern tip of South America

President Bartlett – United States

Natalie – Bartlett's secretary

Lord Robbins – Canadian Ambassador to the United Nations

Prime Minister Langdon – British Prime Minister

Donald Sloan – Director of the CIA

Miss Natalie Granger – Presidential Press Secretary

Suzanne – woman from the New York underground invasion

Tiffin – Suzanne's young son

Jack – guide through the sewers

Phaschin – parrot in the white plane

Thomas Connor - reporter

The Plane of the Animals

Orana – the oldest *seer* on the planet

Unis – female unicorn

Malan – Unis' mate

Legio Obscurum

Zepallo – The Dark Lord – Minister of Cultural Relations of the Council of Ollapez

Ptolemy – Head of the Council – ancient and domineering dark *seer* and Minister of Internal Affairs, lost during the invasion of Morgan's Knot

Wonac –a hulking Dark Master *seer* and Council member – who presided over the military, lost during the invasion of Morgan's Knot

Cadeau - Senior Security Technician – Korean complex

Regis – Senior Regent for Command and Control - Korean complex

The Island of Dark Miracles

Morgan's Knot – A Serial Fantasy
Episode VII

Preview

A woozy Zepallo gazed around the restricted ward in which he was the only patient. The sheets were white. The ceiling, walls, and floor were white. The *orbs* illuminating the room in soothing pools of cool blue spilling across the foot of the bed, the walls beside banks of monitoring systems, and the floor just inside the door, cast the rest of the room into soft gray twilight. The effect reinforced the clinically sterile ambiance and grated on his testy disposition. He struggled to sit up, as The Doctor rushed into the infirmary, a brilliant and determined renegade scientist with a shock of white hair over a pallid complexion, dark deep-set eyes, and a white smock that almost touched the white booties covering his shoes.

The Dark Lord held up the bandaged stump of his right arm, "So our experiment bears fruit?"

"We are fortunate that the Masters chose you to father of the next generation. Although we only had three specimens that qualify as a complete success, we have plenty of spare parts," replied The Doctor in a thick German accent.

"You can harvest a hand, my hand?"

"Of course it will be your hand, with your fingerprints. The only difference is that your new hand will be young and it will develop the strength of a young hand." The Doctor smiled, "and we've added some new...options that you might find useful."

Zepallo scowled.

The Doctor continued with due respect but unabated, "The only frustration is that our ability to generate new life on an accelerated schedule leads to accelerated aging. We're working on the problem but our first generation is years ahead of what we consider a normal chronological scale. Your hand will suffer the same process."

"So the hand will have to be replaced again?"

"Yes. We are estimating ten to fifteen years."

"How quickly are my progeny aging?"

"Our latest calculations indicate that they are growing at approximately three times the normal rate. They will mature at four or five, certainly before the year is out, and have the size, weight, mental capacity, and physical prowess of a legal adult before the age of seven. At twenty-five, they'll qualify for retirement."

"What of the next generation?"

"We're confident that our success rate will increase dramatically and, through a manipulation of the genes that control aging, we hope their maturation will be slowed to about double the normal rate."

"How many new citizens might we hope for?"

"In the next group, I might expect, perhaps, one hundred."

"And the next?"

"We're planning to deliver ten times that number," replied the Doctor, with a confident smile, "but, as always, there are challenges to be met."

"And each will be exactly the same as the next?"

"They will be identical…carbon copies of our Dark Lord."

The patient settled back into his pillows, as The Doctor inserted a hypodermic into the intravenous tube feeding into the Zepallo's veins. The chemicals would take effect within a few minutes and the operation could begin.

"This process could conceivably continue indefinitely. The seeds are sewn for an endless source of reliable, dedicated, and intelligent agents to lead the planet to unification under the Dark Powers…"

Chapter 2

Adrian hovered a foot above the ground, eyes closed, hands resting on his knees, palms open to the sky. It was cool in the shade of the huge oak tree hanging over the edge of the vegetable garden. A gentle wind wafted in off the ocean tussling his blond hair, hanging in soft waves around his tanned face, like the branches of a willow tree…moving with the breeze and then falling back.

The words of his three hundred year old self kept repeating in his head, "Life is filled with joy and wonder. It is everywhere and in everything. It is in every child's smile, every animal that you will encounter, every day that ends without a battle, and every calm moment that you will enjoy. Looking back on it all, I would say that you should be thankful for every normal day. Those days when nothing happens, when you could be bored, when things are confined to everyday routines, those are most precious."

A smile rippled through is mind. The last three months had been calm, allowing time with the people he loved the most. He could honestly say that he found days when he had been bored, in spite of endless chores around the House of the Four Seasons and his work with Alius and the texts at Ponte's observatory, and days when he got to play, like a normal boy, with his friends. The wound on his chest healed enough to dive with Raffe and help with the construction of the first dome. In spite of missing most of the final semester of classes the previous year and having to make up the work, he had enjoyed a real summer vacation.

His mother told him that the tailors would be shutting down the seamstress shop within the next month. Once everyone was fitted, they would only need to repair or replace the diving suits that were damaged or outgrown. Almost everyone on the island completed their training with Soule and Amy and the anticipation of exploring and joining this new undersea world infected the entire population.

The first dome would serve as the primary interface connecting the dry world with the wet. It would also be the new, although temporary, home for the upper school students because the old school building on the ridge was bursting at its seams with students overflowing every classroom, crowding into the canteen in ravenous waves during lunch, even packing the playground and the athletic fields during breaks and after classes. The Headmaster, Dr. Carringsworth, demanded that the first undersea dome be dedicated to providing facilities for the upper school to relieve the congestion. Thus, all of the classes for the upperclassmen, which now included Adrian, Alius, and the twins, were transferred out of the old school building.

The new classrooms were completed the day before the start of classes, although some had yet to receive the finishing touches, but each had an open view of the sea. Most of the students felt that the younger children should have been moved into the new dome, allowing the older children to finish their schooling in the building to which they had grown accustomed. It was a change that disrupted tradition and, although most young people rebel at such things, they still sought to use any change to their advantage in their eternal quest to rile the elders.

~

After dinner, Adrian joined the twins to watch the international news on the *messenger* in their bedroom…he, for the World view, and the twins for a continuing assignment from their political science teacher, Mrs. Hammon, who insisted that her students stay attuned to the political, economic, and social changes happening across the globe. She was known for her pop quizzes posing in depth questions on the latest maneuverings in Washington or Peking, the current political attitude of the oil producing countries, or the impact of an election in some minor nation…and this year, they were to pay special attention to the effects of the children's campaign against war, against the savagery that adults wage upon each other for reasons beyond any child's comprehension.

Adrian turned to his cousins, "Do you realize that, other than terrorists who prey on common citizens for their own weird political purposes, there aren't any wars happening anywhere in the world?"

Megan piped up, "I think they have you to thank for that!"

"Oh, I can't take the credit or the blame, I just spoke the truth and the children of the world did the rest."

"It's too bad that President Bartlett can't run for another term. He was a good president and a true world leader. I wonder who will take his place?"

"The election is two weeks off and the political reporters say that it's dead even," said Molly.

"I wonder what he'll do after he leaves office," pondered Adrian.

"Did you feel that the person that we see on the *messenger* was the person you met?"

Adrian smiled, "He's shorter than he appears on the news but much stronger and even more in command than he seems when he's in public."

"Did you like him?" asked Megan.

"Yeah, I did. I thought he was extremely intelligent and polite, genuine in an old-fashioned sort of way. He listened to our tale and didn't act as if we were just children telling stories and he does have a sense of humor. I'd like to show him the island, especially now that we have the first dome completed. Who knows, maybe after he leaves office, we could convince him to come for a visit."

"Yeah, as if the Secret Service is going to place the security of an ex-president in the hands of a bunch of children and people they can't trace, on an island that doesn't show up on their radar, let alone their maps!" laughed Megan. "That'll never happen."

"Do you know how to get in touch with him?" asked Molly.

"Sure," replied Adrian. "I know his personal Internet address."

"Then you should invite him before he leaves office. I'll bet he'd come!"

"I might just do that…just to prove a point to your Mrs. Hammon. She'd have to give you a passing grade if you brought a president to class," smirked Adrian.

"That might be the only way to get a good grade in her class!" laughed Molly.

"I want to take your class," said Megan.

"Yeah, me too."

"I'm going to be a hard grader because I want all of you to understand the potential of the Powers in everybody's lives. You don't have to be a *seer* or a Keeper to find new ways to use this energy. I think most people on the island have a vague understanding of how it works and they enjoy the benefits but what if everyone really understood it? Then we'd have hundreds of different viewpoints seeing things that none of us might have considered," said Adrian.

The two *seers* had been asked to teach a class together on The Powers. After consulting with Ester and Mary, who knew far more of their history than anyone else, other than Orana, they decided to confine their lessons to those adventures that might serve as examples for the rest of the children to use in their everyday lives. Dadeus and Ponte were working on new curriculum that involved the use of the Powers with marine life in the ocean but the *seer's* class took a far more human approach.

Their first lesson brought more than a bit of trepidation. They were still students with the other children for the rest of each day but they were the teachers during this one course and wanted to give their friends something more than they received in most of their other classes.

After long discussions, they decided to start with something that Shambala said before Adrian's speech to the United Nations. "We teach our children that if you truly believe that you can do something…say fly…you might not have the ability now but your belief will drive your curiosity and it will lead you to find a way to make it real. Taking it to its finest level, belief is enough to create reality."

On the first day of classes, Adrian and Alius allowed their students to enter the classroom, which was on the third level, before levitating through the door behind them, flying over their heads, and hovering above a small riser at the front of the classroom.

The students were awestruck, standing motionless with their mouths hanging open.

The young instructors descended to the floor and Alius said, with complete confidence, "Why don't you sit down and we'll tell you about The Powers?"

The students took their chairs without a word.

Adrian stepped to the front of the little stage and spoke, "Our demonstration was not intended to show off our powers for your amusement. It was my personal reminder that, until a year and half ago, I didn't know that I had any special talents or that I might be called upon to do the things that I have been asked to do. I was a normal kid, just like each of you."

He looked around the room at the students, who were enthralled with his every word. "The point is that each of us has a unique set of powers and talents. Every one of you is capable of doing at least one thing that I could not possibly accomplish and, yet, they're second nature and you do them with ease."

Pointing to Eloise, a heavy-set girl with dark curly hair, a pale complexion, and lips that curled into a most beautiful smile, he said, "Eloise, you can play the flute and you can make absolutely beautiful music. That's a talent that none of the rest of us has. And Hector," He pointed to a small boy with red hair, blues eyes, and an impish grin, "You can run faster than any other boy on the island. No one can catch you. Almy, you get the best grades in the school. The rest of us try to complete but you always come out on top."

"Do you see what I'm saying?" He paused. "Each of you has talents and abilities that make you unique and special. Be proud of those gifts, work hard to develop them, and use them well.

"We have no proof…but we believe that some of the things that we've learned to do, could be done by anyone. Some of these seemingly magical talents are not confined to those who are born a *seer* or study to become a Keeper."

Alius interrupted, "We talked and talked about how to present our view of The Powers to you in a way that would make sense and help you to reach for your own potential. We agreed that our lessons should be based on something that a friend of ours told us…and that was, that you might not be able to accomplish everything that you dream of doing, at least not now. But, if you truly believe, that energy and determination will lead you to pursue your dreams and, perhaps someday, allow you to find the path to fulfillment. She said, 'Taking this idea to its finest level, belief is enough to create reality'."

With that, Simian strode into the room, dressed in a beautiful patterned yellow sash that wrapped around his upper body. He wore blue pantaloon pants made from the same material that Sara and Morgan had bought in his little stall in Jamaica, during their trip to the Island of Children, and bright pink shoes that curled up at the toes. His little glasses hung precariously on the end of his broad nose and his goatee seemed whiter than before he returned to Jamaica after Adrian's speech.

The old Jamaican carried a bundle of goose feathers in a woven shoulder bag, which leaked white fluff that floated to the floor like a wispy veil trailing in his wake. He smiled at the students, "Good afternoon, I'm pleased to be here with you!"

Alius took Simian's arm and said, "Many of the things that we've learned came at the instruction of our friend Simian, a *seer* from Jamaica."

Simian turned to the students with a huge smile, "I want to talk with you about the power that lives inside seemingly inanimate things. There is energy in everything around us…the trees, the rocks, the ocean…" He turned and waved at the spectacular view of sunlight streaming through the water behind him. "The ocean pulses with its own rhythm. Certainly, the tides are governed by the movements of the moon and the waves are the product of the winds but, if you look beyond the obvious scientific explanations, it is the birthplace for all life. Our ancient ancestors crawled out of the sea onto the shore, where they changed and evolved over the eons to become us!"

"Everything has its own energy and we are affected by the energies around us. Each of you gives off a charge that is unique to you. We call it an aura, an energy field that surrounds everything and everyone…but that is another lecture!"

He pulled a large white feather from his bag and held it in the palm of his hand. "This feather has no weight."

He blew hard and the feather leapt into the air and spiraled to the floor. "It is in its nature to fly!"

Retrieving the feather, he held it up to the class. "This feather lifted a heavy bird into the air and carried it for hundreds, if not, thousands of miles. It is strong and sturdy, ingeniously crafted to flex in several directions without breaking, and perfectly curved to provide lift. It wants to fly, even if there is no wind."

He concentrated on the white feather in his hand and, slowly, it began to flutter, rising several inches above his palm to fan his face, before returning to rest on his fingertips. The students stared in wonder.

Simian smiled and said softly, "It was not my energy that made it fly. That energy already exists inside the feather. I merely gave it permission."

Everyone laughed, as Simian moved from one desk to the next, plucking feathers from his bag and handing one to each student. He returned to the riser at the front of the classroom, with a wink to Adrian and Alius. "I want each of you to hold your feather on the tips of your fingers and then blow on it gently, give it just enough air to provide lift."

The students puffed at their feathers, which flew into the air, a blizzard spinning down to the floor, as if some giant goose had flown through the room, shedding softy puffy down snowflakes.

"Now let's see whether each of you can allow the feather to show its true character. Don't try to make it fly…allow it to use the air. Hold it on your palm. Concentrate on the fact that it wants to fly. It's in its nature and the only thing holding it back is your hand. Set it free!"

Most of the feathers spiraled to the floor but every child picked them up and tried again and again. There were fierce stares, as they concentrated on the essence of their feathers but none showed any frustration when the experiment did not supply instant gratification.

Simian spotted Eloise at the back of the room and her feather floating just above the palm of her hand, as she whispered and coaxed it into the air. "Ah, I see that one of you has found the magic. The young lady with the dark hair in the back, everyone look, she's done it!"

The rest of the students gathered around the heavy-set girl. "I thought that maybe there was a musical tone that would fit with my feather, so I started humming to it, trying to find the right vibration, and suddenly it started to rise, all by itself!"

There were comments and whispers throughout the group, "If she can do it, then I can too!" and several more made their feathers fly before the young teachers had to dismiss the class for the day.

Simian raised his hands for the attention of the students, "This is a preliminary demonstration. With some practice, more of you will master this challenge. I'll come back and we will learn a bit more the next time."

The students applauded and reluctantly moved on to their next classes.

Adrian and Alius hugged their friend, "That was brilliant!" said Alius, "I think we were both reminded of our hesitation and disbelief when you first taught us about levitation. We really appreciate your help."

"Ah, it is my pleasure," laughed the little Jamaican. "What's brilliant is that the authorities in this school have allowed you to conduct this class! The rest of the students will certainly benefit from the things that you have experienced."

"How's Sammy?" asked Adrian.

"He's fine. In fact, he's at the observatory, as we speak. He has a long list of questions for the Professor and Nanchez, and now Dadeus, about using the vectors to supply electrical power. Although our country is modern in many ways, there are many poor people who live in conditions that are shameful at best. They lack power and fresh clean water, let alone a sewer. He wants to construct a small experimental network to help those people."

"That's wonderful," commented Alius. "The Powers should benefit the common people, not the rich corporations!"

"I believe that he'll be successful but we'll have to find a way to construct this network without raising the suspicion of the authorities. They might wonder why shanties have lights and power without being connected to their grid and accuse these poor people of stealing their precious electricity."

"I can see the problem," said Adrian. "It was hard for me to believe that *orbs* could provide light without being connected to wires or batteries or whatever, that cars could move along the paths without proper engines, or that the three-dimensional images we see on the *messengers* are not available in the rest of the world. All of it is still rather amazing."

"I agree," said Simian. "Considering some of what we've learned from Dadeus and some of the other Keepers, I might guess that we're only using a small part of the potential of the Crystals."

Adrian laughed, "As Ponte always says, 'there's always more to learn about the Powers!'"

Simian smiled knowingly and placed his gnarled hand on the young *seer's* shoulder, "We all know he speaks the truth."

Chapter 3

Zepallo inspected his new hand. It was young. The skin was taut and unmarked. The long slender fingers extended and flexed smoothly, his knuckles were like a series of well-lubricated gears, and it looked exactly like his left hand. He was amazed by the thin red line around his arm, above the wrist, that marked the junction between his old body and his new appendage.

The Doctor wrapped a bandage around the healing wound, leaving the hand free and unbound. "It will take several weeks to regain your normal strength and coordination. You'll begin your therapy this afternoon where you'll also learn how to use several new devices that we've incorporated for your added…protection."

"I don't understand."

"For several years, I've been working on a personal weapon that could channel the Powers through the human body. After all, we are controlled by electrical impulses and they are the result of chemical reactions. The energy of the Crystals is very much the same as the energy that controls our bodies. I have merely adjusted the frequency."

He took the Dark Lord's new hand and extended the index finger, pointing it towards an eye chart on the far wall. He pressed the first knuckle and the tip of his finger glowed the bluish white of a superheated flame. An electrical charge surged across the room, shredding the paper into tiny fragments that showered the floor in flames.

"You'll learn to use this by merely thinking about it. Obviously, we would rather that you not indulge your curiosity until we have had a chance to work with you and to fine tune the instrument."

Zepallo stared at The Doctor. "That's incredible. I felt the surge flow down my arm and out through my finger!"

"I thought you might enjoy the…convenience."

"You said 'new devices.' What other options did you add?"

"Well, the other obvious improvement is that we have made some modifications to the tendons and ligaments that will allow your right hand to be several times stronger than your left," smiled The Doctor. "Please do not experiment with it yet. Just as you learned to use your original hand and developed your strength and coordination through a series of repetitive demands over time, we will teach you to reach an optimum level in short order."

"I'll try to be patient…but tell me about the charge. I want to understand it."

The Doctor smiled modestly, "As my little demonstration showed, it's very similar in intensity to the blast that you might fire from your ring, with a range of perhaps twelve to fifteen meters but, in my experiments, I've noticed that when it is used in close combat, it leaves no mark on the skin."

"That could be very useful."

"A charge of this magnitude, applied to the chest would result in violent fluctuations of the rhythm of the heart muscles or total paralysis, without leaving any evidence on the surface."

They both inspected the raised hand as if it were a piece of sculpture. The Dark Lord stared at his physician, "I want to see my offspring."

The Doctor smiled again, "I've been wanting to show them to you for quite some time but I felt that it would be better when they had completed some of their training and…your mere presence would disrupt our research. Now, I believe that time has come. Are you feeling up to a short stroll?"

Zepallo put his feet on the floor and stood up. He wavered for a moment as he readjusted his sense of balance, which suffered as a result of the anesthetics and his confinement. He arched his back, stretched, and placing his new hand on The Doctor's shoulder, "I've shown great restraint since the program's inception because you must learn how to develop the children to achieve their potentials but I must admit that I've been anxious to see the results. Shall we go?"

The two men walked through the sterile white hallways of the complex that had been nestled into the corals beneath an uncharted island in the Savu Sea along the southern archipelago of the islands of Indonesia. Research, development, and living quarters were attached to a central ring encircling a hub that contained a giant Black Crystal. To satellites that photographed every square inch of the planet, as they swept through their orbits every ninety minutes, this facility appeared an integral part of a corral reef.

The Doctor said, "We chose this spot because it is easy to maintain the necessary temperatures for our production without excessive cooling or heating. As we learned, pearls and human embryos require similar conditions. Our systems filter and purify millions of gallons of salt water, which provides a perfect medium, and our test facility is kept at a constant 98.6 degrees Fahrenheit, the temperature of the human body."

He tapped a code into a tiny *messenger* on a wall and the door slid back to reveal a glass tunnel to a darkened circular control station with a three hundred and sixty degree view. Water flowed through the tank outside the glass sphere, swaying thousands of bulbous tubes, each pulsing with an iridescent green glow. The Doctor waved his hand around the circle of the giant incubator. "At the moment, these embryos are in various stages of development and, when we have perfected our program, we can easily expand to produce ten times this number."

"And all of these came from a small sample that was taken from me all those years ago?"

"Yes, we've replicated your DNA many times. That information is introduced into a fertilized egg that is grown in perfect conditions in our facility. After nine months, a child is born and moved to our nursery. It will be cared for by trained nurses and gradually introduced to our educational program, which is still under development. As I said earlier, their progress is rather astonishing, maturing at three times the normal rate. Our first subjects would be about twelve or thirteen now. As you will see they are not like most twelve year olds."

"I believe this qualifies as a miracle, a dark miracle."

They walked back to the corridor and turned into another glass tunnel open to sunlight streaming down through the sea. The two men entered an observation deck above a pod that had been constructed for the youngsters. From their vantage point, they could see the living quarters, a small classroom with multiple *messengers*, laboratory equipment, and a library of books surrounding a large gymnasium that rose two stories, with ropes, wires, and climbing walls, as well as an interface to the open water.

Five divers emerged from the ocean and walked up a shallow ramp. The two larger divers were obviously instructors. The shorter three, although well-muscled for their age, pulled off their helmets to reveal identical features. Long dark hair framed the pale skin of a slender face. High cheekbones made their intense blue eyes appear recessed slightly into their skulls. A fierce, ominous glare sparkled in the shadows beneath their eyebrows as each stopped to stare at the darkened observation pod.

Zepallo's jaw dropped open. He recognized those eyes, those faces from a lifetime of staring into a mirror. They were exactly as he had been when he was twelve...physically...and he could feel their energies probing his own. "What do you call them?" He whispered.

"Alpha, Beta, and Gamma."

"Are they truly identical?"

"Physically, yes, but each has a slightly different personality. Alpha is the first to step forward when there is any sort of challenge. Beta is a bit more standoffish...he likes to size up the situation before deciding on a course of action. Where Alpha might rush into a hasty decision, Beta would have thought the problem through and come up with a reasonable response. Gamma is quiet, a bit withdrawn, and far more emotional and organized than his brothers."

"Considering they all came from the same genes, they have lived together and received similar treatment and instruction, why would they be different in their manner?"

"One simple answer might be sibling rivalry. Put any group of subjects together in a confined space, especially under adverse conditions, and they will establish, without prompting, their pecking order. Who is the strongest, who is the weakest, and who claims those places in between? It is the law of nature and each adapts to their role."

Zepallo stared at the clones. Each of them an exact copy, yet each was different, unique. He considered his past and realized that he could have been any of them. Alpha, standing ramrod straight, his hands moving as he talked...from his manner, it appeared that he was giving instructions. Beta was relaxed, his weight rested on his right leg, while his left was slightly bent. He leaned back and hooked his thumbs into a strap around the waist of his diving suit, with a look of mild amusement in his blue eyes and the curve of his slender lips. Gamma was busy arranging the equipment lying on the platform, ignoring his brothers. He would willingly work with the others but he would not hesitate to make conquests on his own.

"A leader in battle, a tactician, and an organizational genius. Each useful in their own unique way." The Doctor smiled, "They possess your gifts but each will make use of an individual set of talents that will define their identities. I thought that you would be pleased."

"Are they equal in all other ways?"

"Yes. They are all extraordinary students, each excelling in different areas but brilliant none-the-less. Although Alpha is physically dominant, Beta focuses and tames his enthusiasm, while Gamma maintains equilibrium and controls everything in the background. They're a team and, when our next generation is born, I think that we should consider organizing them into family groups like this. Having grown up together and being trained as a unit, they'll work seamlessly, employing their own mental telepathy, which should prove to be extremely useful."

"I've been feeling their communications since I arrived in this facility." He saluted the physician, "You're a genius!"

The Doctor bowed.

"I'd like to see them in the field and I think I might have the perfect test subject for them to execute the skills that you've taught them. We'll need some bait to draw him out of his sanctuary," smiled Zepallo, holding up his new hand like a trophy.

The adventure continues in

The Island of Dark Miracles

Morgan's Knot - A Serial Fantasy
Episode VII

The seeds are sewn for an endless supply of reliable, dedicated, and intelligent agents to lead the planet to unification under the Dark Powers...and they will all be identical carbon copies of our Dark Lord.

Visit: www.morgansknot.com

Eric T. Stiller is the author of the Morgan's Knot Serial Fantasy, as well as several new adult novels. He is an award-winning commercial photographer, an educator and advocate, and a Master Gardener.

Visit: www.rickstiller.com for more of his work.

If you enjoyed this story, please give it a five-star review on my Amazon sales page and like my 'Eric T Stiller — Author' page on Facebook.